Lynne Graham

THE SPANISH BILLIONAIRE'S PREGNANT WIFE

BRIDES *Virgin* ♥ HUSBANDS *Arrogant*

HARLEQUIN®

TORONTO • NEW YORK • LONDON
AMSTERDAM • PARIS • SYDNEY • HAMBURG
STOCKHOLM • ATHENS • TOKYO • MILAN • MADRID
PRAGUE • WARSAW • BUDAPEST • AUCKLAND

Recycling programs
for this product may
not exist in your area.

ISBN-13: 978-0-373-12795-5
ISBN-10:   0-373-12795-2

THE SPANISH BILLIONAIRE'S PREGNANT WIFE

First North American Publication 2009.

Copyright © 2008 by Lynne Graham.

This is a work of fiction. Names, characters, places and incidents are either the product of the author's imagination or are used fictitiously, and any resemblance to actual persons, living or dead, business establishments, events or locales is entirely coincidental.

This edition published by arrangement with Harlequin Books S.A.

® and TM are trademarks of the publisher. Trademarks indicated with ® are registered in the United States Patent and Trademark Office, the Canadian Trade Marks Office and in other countries.

www.eHarlequin.com

Printed in U.S.A.

All about the author…
Lynne Graham

Of Irish/Scottish parentage, **LYNNE GRAHAM** has lived in Northern Ireland all her life. She has one brother. She grew up in a seaside village and now lives in a country house surrounded by a woodland garden, which is wonderfully private.

Lynne first met her husband when she was fourteen. They married after she completed a degree at Edinburgh University. Lynne wrote her first book at fifteen and it was rejected everywhere. She started writing again when she was home with her first child. It took several attempts before she sold her first book, and the delight of seeing that book for sale in the local newsagents has never been forgotten.

Lynne always wanted a large family, and she has five children. Her eldest and her only natural child is in her twenties and is a university graduate. Her other children, who are every bit as dear to her heart, are adopted: two from Sri Lanka and two from Guatemala. In Lynne's home, there is a rich and diverse cultural mix, which adds a whole extra dimension of interest and discovery to family life.

The family has two pets. Thomas, a very large and affectionate black cat, bosses the dog and hunts rabbits. The dog is Daisy, an adorable but not very bright West Highland white terrier, who loves being chased by the cat. At night, dog and cat sleep together in front of the kitchen stove.

Lynne loves gardening and cooking, collects everything from old toys to rock specimens and is crazy about every aspect of Christmas.

CHAPTER ONE

LEANDRO CARRERA MARQUEZ, Duque de Sandoval, awoke when his valet opened the bedroom curtains and bid his illustrious employer a cheerful good morning. His lean, darkly handsome face grim, Leandro doubted that the day ahead would be the slightest bit different from any other day in recent months. Fresh towels were laid out in the bathroom for his shower. A custom-made designer business suit and a monogrammed silk shirt and toning tie were assembled in readiness for his getting dressed.

Elegant and, as always, immaculate in appearance, Leandro finally descended the magnificent staircase of the family *castillo* with all the cool assurance and dignity of his grand forebears. He knew that he was bored and he scorned the feeling, well aware that he was bountifully blessed with health, wealth and success. The walls he passed bore the portraits of his predecessors—the very flower of proud Castilian aristocracy—ranging from the first duke, who had been a famous soldier and a contemporary of Christopher Columbus, to Leandro's father, a distinguished banker who had died when his son was barely five years old.

'Your Excellency.' Having been greeted by Basilio, his major-domo, and two maidservants at the foot of the stairs with much the same pomp and ceremony that the first duque would have received in the fifteenth century, Leandro was ushered into breakfast where the day's papers, including the leading financial publications, awaited him. There was no need for him to ask for anything. His every need and wish were carefully foreseen by his devoted staff and perfect peace reigned while he ate, for his preference for silence at the breakfast table was well known.

A phone was brought to him. His mother, the dowager Duquesa, Doña Maria, was on the line asking him to lunch with her at the town house in Seville later that day. It didn't suit him. He would have to reschedule business appointments at the bank. But Leandro, uneasily aware that he spent little time with his relations, gave reluctant assent.

As he sipped his coffee his brilliant dark eyes rested on the full-length portrait of his late wife, Aloise, on the wall at the other end of the room. He wondered if anyone else in the family even appreciated that in forty-eight hours the anniversary of Aloise's death would take place. Aloise, his childhood friend, who in dying almost a year earlier had left a gaping hole in the settled fabric of his life. He wondered if he would ever get over the guilt induced by her tragic demise and decided that it would be wise to spend that day away from home working in London. Sentimentality was not one of Leandro's failings.

He spent a very busy morning at the Carrera Bank, an institution that had been handling the same clients' fortunes for generations and where his own services as one of the financial world's most fabulously successful investment bankers were much in demand. Strikingly intelligent and gifted in the field of wealth preservation and asset management, Leandro had been marked out early as a genius at analysing world money markets. Juggling complex figures gave him considerable pleasure and satisfaction. Numbers, unlike people, were easy to understand and deal with, he acknowledged wryly.

When he kept his luncheon appointment he was surprised to see that his mother's sister, his aunt Isabella, and his own two sisters, Estefania and Julieta, were also present.

'I felt that it was time to talk to you,' Doña Maria murmured with a meaningful look at her only son over the appetisers.

Leandro elevated a questioning ebony brow. 'About what, precisely?'

'You've been a widower for a year now.' It was Estefania who responded.

'Is there a point to that obvious statement?' Leandro enquired drily.

'You've spent enough time in mourning to satisfy the conventions. It's time to think of remarriage,' his mother informed him.

His lean, strong face rigidly controlled, Leandro stared steadily back at the older woman. 'I don't agree.'

Julieta, his younger sister piped up, 'Nobody is going to replace Aloise, Leandro. We don't expect that and neither can you—'

'But you must put the family's unbroken line of inheritance first,' Doña Maria declared with gravity. 'There is presently no heir to the title or the estate. You are thirty-three years old. Last year when Aloise died we all learned how fragile and fickle life can be. What if something similar were to happen to you? You *must* remarry and father an heir, my son.'

Leandro compressed his handsome mouth into a bloodless line that would have encouraged less determined opponents to drop the subject. He had no need of such reminders when he had spent his life being made aware daily of his many responsibilities. Indeed he had never known an hour's freedom from the weighty burden of expectations that accompanied his privileged social status and great wealth. He had been raised in the same traditions as his ancestors to put duty and honour and family first. But an exceptional spark of rebellion was finally firing inside his lean, well built body.

'I'm aware of those facts, but I'm not ready to take another wife,' he retorted crisply.

'I thought it would be helpful if we drew up a short list of potential brides to help you,' Doña Maria contended with a wide smile that struck her angry son as bordering on manic.

'I don't think that would be helpful. Indeed I think it's a ludicrous idea,' Leandro replied coldly. 'When and *if* I remarry, I will choose my own wife.'

His aunt Isabella, however, would not be silenced. She put forward a candidate from a family as rich and prominent as their own. Leandro dealt her a look of scorn. His mother was, however, even quicker to name her own selection—a young widow with a son and, therefore, what the older woman termed a *proven* fertility record. An expression of unhidden distaste crossed Leandro's classic dark features. He knew exactly why that point was being made. Unhappily, talk of fertility records reminded him of livestock breeding. His elder sister, Estefania, was not to be outdone and, oblivious to the disbelieving glances of her relations, suggested the teenaged daughter of a personal friend as being perfect bride material. Leandro almost laughed out loud at that idea. As he was well aware, marriage could be a most challenging relationship, even for those who might seem very well matched as a couple.

'We'll hold a party and invite some suitable women,' Doña Maria announced, continuing on her theme with the stubborn insensitivity of a woman determined to have her say. 'But not the teenager, Estefania. I really don't think so young a woman would be appropriate. A Marquez bride needs to be mature, well versed in etiquette, educated and socially accomplished, as well as being from a suitable background.'

'I will not attend any such party,' Leandro declared without hesitation. 'I have no intention of remarrying at this point in time.'

Julieta gave him an apologetic look. 'But at least if you went to the party you might fall in love with someone.'

'Leandro is the Duque de Sandoval,' Doña Maria countered in a deflating tone of ice. 'Thankfully, he knows who he is and he has no nonsense of that variety in his head.'

'There will be no party,' Leandro decreed, implacable outrage igniting steadily beneath his cool façade at their comments. He could hardly credit that his own relations could be so crass or interfering. But then he was willing to admit that none of them was close. The formality and reserve that his mother had always insisted on had driven wedges of polite behaviour between them all.

'We are only thinking of you and what is best for you,' Doña Maria murmured sweetly.

Leandro studied the woman who had sent him to an English boarding school at the age of six years old and remained impervious to his tear-stained letters begging to be allowed to come home. 'I know what is best for me, Mama. A man must act for himself in such a personal matter.'

'Happy birthday, Molly! What do you think?' Jez Andrews prompted, standing back from the car with a flourish.

Wide-eyed, Molly Chapman studied her elderly car. Jez had repainted it a cerise pink colour that she loved on sight. She walked round the vehicle, stunned by a transformation that had caused all the rust, dents and scratches to disappear. 'It's amazing! You've worked a miracle, Jez.'

'That's what mates are for. Hopefully it'll pass the MOT test now without any major problems. I've replaced a lot of parts. I knew that helping you to keep your car on the road was the best present I could give you,' her friend and landlord admitted.

Molly flung her arms round him in an exuberant hug. A stocky fair-haired man of medium height, Jez was still a comfortable seven inches taller than Molly, who was tiny in stature and build, with a mop of dark curls and enormous green eyes. Her quick graceful movements crackled with the energy of a lively personality. 'I don't know how to thank you.'

Jez shrugged and backed off, embarrassed by her gratitude. 'It was no big deal,' he said awkwardly.

But Molly knew the full value of his generosity and it touched her to the heart that he had sacrificed so much of his free time to work on her beat-up car. But then, Jez was her closest friend and he knew that she needed the vehicle to get round the craft shops and fairs where she sold her wares at weekends. Molly and Jez had been in foster care together as children and their ties went back a long way.

'Don't forget I'm staying over at Ida's tonight,' Jez reminded her. 'I'll see you tomorrow.'

'How is Ida?'

At the thought of the sick older woman, Jez vented a sad sigh. 'About as well as can be expected. I mean, it's not like she's going to get any better.'

'Any word of her getting into the hospice yet?'

'No, but she's top of the list.'

Thinking how typical it was of Jez to be helping to nurse the woman who had fostered him for a while in his teens, Molly went back indoors. It was almost time for her to go to work. Jez had inherited his terraced house and garden in Hackney from a bachelor uncle. That piece of good fortune had enabled him to finance and set up a car repair shop where he was currently making a comfortable living. Jez had been quick to offer Molly a bedsit in his home and the valuable opportunity to use the stone shed in the back garden to house her potter's kiln.

Success, however, had so far eluded Molly. She had left art college with such high hopes of the future, but even though she worked every hour she could for the catering company that employed her she still struggled to pay the rent and keep up with her bills. Her dream was to sell enough of her ceramics, which she made in her spare time, to make it worth her while to work full-time as a potter, and she often felt like a failure in the artistic stakes because she never seemed to get any closer to achieving her goal.

Like Jez, Molly had had a chequered background, which had encompassed constant change, broken relationships and insecurity. Her mother had died when she was nine years old and her grandmother had put her up for adoption while choosing to keep Ophelia, Molly's elder teenaged sister. Molly had never quite recovered from the simple fact that her own flesh and blood had handed her over to social services simply because she, unlike her sister, was illegitimate and, even worse, the embarrassing proof of her mother's affair with a married man. The sheer hurt of that unapologetic rejection had made Molly wary of trying to seek contact with her birth relations again once she grew up. Even now, at the age of twenty-two, she tended to block out the memories of the early years of her life and scold herself for the sense of loss that those dim recollections still roused. Molly was a survivor who, while priding herself on being as tough as old boots, had a heart as soft as a marshmallow.

That evening, her employers were catering for a wedding party at a big house in St John Wood. It was an upmarket booking for a new customer and her manager, Brian, was very anxious to get everything right. Molly tied her apron on over the narrow black skirt and white blouse that she wore for work. The bride's mother, Krystal Forfar, an enervated and emaciated blonde dressed in an oyster-pink dress, was rapping out imperious instructions to Brian in a shrill voice.

Brian signalled Molly. 'My senior waitress, Molly… There'll be a bloke here tonight—'

'Mr Leandro Carrera Marquez,' the bride's mother

interposed haughtily, pronouncing the foreign name in the sort of hallowed tones that most people reserved for royalty. 'He's a Spanish banker and, as my husband's employer, our most important guest. Make sure you wait on him hand and foot. Ensure his glass is never empty. I'll point him out when he arrives.'

'Fine.' Molly nodded acquiescence and sped off back to the kitchen where she was helping to unpack equipment.

'What was all that about?' Vanessa, her fellow waitress, asked.

Molly explained.

'Another toff with more money than sense, I'll bet,' the redhead opined.

'If he's a banker, it's to be hoped he has both!' Molly joked.

The bride, stunning in a sophisticated sheath of white satin, appeared with her mother to check the buffet table. Molly watched while Mrs Forfar fussed over her daughter, twitching her train into place and adjusting her tiara. Unappreciative of the proud parental attention she was receiving, the bride uttered a sharp complaint about the colour of the napkins—*so* last year and not what she had ordered. Brian surged forward to apologise and explain the substitution, while Molly wondered why she herself had failed to win her mother's love, and why the only affection she had received during the first nine years of her life had been from her sister. Had her mother been so ashamed of her illegitimacy as well?

A few minutes later, Molly was summoned to the doorway to have the Spanish banker singled out for her scrutiny. The tall dark male engaged in conversation with the bride's parents was so breathtakingly good looking that Molly felt her heart jump inside her chest as she studied him. He was downright dazzling, from the crown of his fashionably cropped black hair to the flawless planes of his classic bronzed features, and he was further blessed with the sleek, broad-shouldered, lean-hipped and long limbed muscular physique of a classical god.

'Go offer the VIP a drink,' Brian urged.

Molly snatched in a ragged breath, shaken and embarrassed by her excessively appreciative reaction to the Spaniard. It wasn't like her. She had never been into men in the same way as her peers. Her birth mother's volatile relationships with a long line of men who had treated her badly had left their mark on Molly even at a young age. She had known even then that she wanted something different for herself, something more than casual sex with men who didn't want to commit, contribute to the home or play any real part in a child's upbringing. And she didn't want to be hurt or damaged, either. With the exception of Jez, the sort of men Molly had met in the years that took her to adulthood had merely increased her wariness and distrust of the opposite sex. There had been boyfriends but nobody special; certainly nobody she had had any desire to sleep with. So it was a total shock to look across a room and see a guy who, just by being there, stole all the breath from her lungs and all the sense from her thoughts.

The closer Molly got with her tray of drinks, the taller the Spaniard seemed to get and her curious gaze rested on him, greedily noting every detail of his stylish sophisticated appearance. His suit had the classic tailoring and sheen of the most expensive design and the highest quality. He looked rich to her and more as if he *owned* a bank than worked in one.

'Sir?' Molly extended the tray and spoke to gain his attention. He gazed down at her and she discovered that he had wonderfully thick sooty eyelashes for a man and eyes the colour of hot golden honey. Meeting those glorious eyes, she felt as dizzy as if she were suddenly falling from a height.

'Thank you.' Leandro accepted a glass and drank thirstily, for his mouth was very dry. Had it not been for the fact that the Forfars were also close friends of his mother's, he would have definitely stayed at home that evening. A throat infection and a course of antibiotics were making Leandro feel under par. His conscience would have found it a challenge, however, not to show up even for the evening party when he had already successfully avoided attending the actual wedding. In the mood to be alone, he had also given his usual entourage of chauffeur and bodyguards a night off and had driven himself out.

His attention rested on the bridal couple, who were clearly engaged in a dispute, which gave the bride a shrewish look and the groom the pitiful air of a discomfited man wishing he were anywhere but where he was. Leandro knew that feeling. He didn't like weddings either. The artificial jollity left him cold and the divorce statistics made nonsense of the romantic frills and the heartfelt promises. He could not imagine *ever* wanting to marry again and cherished his freedom from that constraint.

Picking her way through the knots of chattering guests, Molly was taken aback when she caught the tall, dark handsome banker's gaze resting on her face.

She went pink, wondered why he looked so forbidding and could not resist smiling in the hope of cheering him up.

The little waitress's sunny smile was as enchanting as her face, Leandro acknowledged, the dark mood that had overtaken him lightening at that fresh sight of her. Almond-shaped green eyes like a cat's sparkled above an unrepentantly upturned nose, dimples and a ripe rosy mouth with a pronounced Cupid's bow. The instant he registered that he was staring, he questioned what he was doing and directed his attention back to the drink in his hand. But, strangely, all he could still see were those bright feline eyes and that marvellously full pink mouth that contrived to combine her curious mix of girlish innocence and feline sex appeal with astonishing efficiency. He was surprised at himself and even more disturbed by the sexual heat stirring him, for he had not been with a woman since Aloise had died. Guilt had killed his libido as surely as death had claimed his wife.

'Over here, luv!' a bold voice called.

Molly hastened to serve drinks at a greater speed for the reception rooms were steadily filling up. A trio of young men who had evidently already enjoyed a few drinks made frank comments about her curvaceous figure as she served them. She gritted her teeth and ignored the over-familiar cracks, walking away as soon as she could. She went back to the bar to collect more orders.

'The VIP's got an empty glass,' Brian warned her anxiously. 'Look after him.'

Molly tried not to look at the banker this time, but her heart was thumping even as she walked across the room towards him. The sense of anticipation and the craving were too great a temptation for her and she surrendered and looked at him again: he really was *gorgeous*, his black hair gleaming below the down lighters that accentuated his superb high cheekbones and hard masculine jaw line. Her mouth ran dry, helpless longing piercing her like a cruel thorn being driven into her flesh.

The power of what she was feeling shocked her. He was a stranger and she knew nothing about him, would most assuredly have nothing whatsoever in common with him. It was a purely physical craving but almost irresistible in its pulling power. For the first time she wondered if something similar had drawn her late mother to her married father and if she herself was guilty of being meanly narrow-minded and unsympathetic in despising her parent for getting involved in an extra-marital affair.

Leandro watched her walking back to him, marvelling at how dainty she was—a pocket Venus with childsized feet and a waist he could probably clasp his hands around. She seemed to move in time to the music. *Dios mio!* What was wrong with him? She was a waitress and not fair game; he was not the sort of low life who hit on serving staff. But his wayward gaze remained stubbornly nailed to her surprisingly voluptuous proportions, noticing the tight fit of her shirt over her round little breasts and the peach-like curve and sensual jut of her bottom below her skirt. Her curling lashes lifted, her green eyes looking up direct into his. He felt the jolt of connection like an electric shock travelling through his lean, powerful frame to set off a chain reaction in his groin. He set down his empty glass on the tray she extended and lifted another drink. For a moment it crossed his mind that his thirst might be more wisely quenched with water than alcohol, but what happened next turned his thoughts in a different direction.

Hailed by the same noisy clique of men she had served earlier, Molly walked over. They read her name off her identification badge and called her by it. One man made a crude comment about her breasts, while she went rigid as another closed an arm round her, trapping her in place.

'Let go of me!' Molly told the offender with icy contempt and annoyance. 'I'm here to serve drinks— that's *all*!'

'What a crying waste that would be, little lady,' the red-faced male imprisoning her lamented. Unconcerned by her angry reproach, he tossed a high-denomination bank note down on the tray. 'Why don't you come home with me later? Trust me, I could show you a really good time.'

'No, thanks. Get your hands off me right now,' Molly demanded.

'Have you any idea how much I earned this year?'

'I couldn't care less and I don't want the tip,' Molly told him curtly, stuffing the note back into his hand and pulling free the instant his grip loosened. How dared he speak to her as if she were a hooker for hire and try to bribe her into doing his bidding? She walked away quickly to the accompaniment of a chorus of male laughter. Brian was watching her uneasily from the doorway and she went straight over to him to warn him that he needed to keep an eye on the rowdy group before they got completely out of hand.

'I won't stand for being touched or spoken to like that. I'm entitled to make a complaint when someone does that to me,' Molly pointed out angrily.

Dismay at that threat sent the manager's brows flying up below his hair. 'Those blokes are only fooling around and trying to flirt with you. You're a pretty girl and there aren't many here. They've had too much to drink. I'm sure nothing offensive was intended.'

'I disagree. They didn't care and I found their abuse deeply offensive,' Molly countered and stalked back to the bar, furious that her complaint was not being taken seriously. She was well aware that the manager was keen to avoid any unpleasantness that might endanger the chance of new business from any of the well-heeled guests present. But for the first time ever, Molly resented her lowly station in life which evidently made Brian feel that her complaint was of less importance than the comfort of the arrogant ignorant oiks who had insulted her.

Leandro drew in a slow deep breath of restraint. He had witnessed the whole scene and had almost intervened on her behalf with the drunks. He thought her boss should have protected her from such harassment. So her name was Molly—he had overheard the men. Wasn't that a diminutive for Mary? And if it was, why the hell should it matter to him? he asked himself in exasperation. He didn't like the feeling that he was off balance. Accompanied by his hostess, Krystal, Leandro allowed himself to be introduced to some of the other guests.

Lysander Metaxis was present without his wife whom, he readily explained, was close to giving birth to their third child. If he was looking for congratulations he didn't get them. When children entered the conversation, Leandro had nothing to say and even less interest. But he did wonder if it was fair of him to suspect that the macho Greek tycoon was boasting about his virility.

There was nothing to distract Leandro from watching Molly as she approached the drunks who were signalling her for more libation. Tension was etched in her tight heart-shaped features and her reluctance to respond was clear. The heavily built blond man snaked out an arm to entrap her again and ran a coarse hand down over her shapely derrière, pausing to squeeze it. As an angry objection erupted from Molly Leandro was already striding forward.

'Take your hands off her!' Leandro commanded.

The drunk freed Molly and pushed her aside to take a swing at the Spaniard. Shaken that Leandro had come to her rescue, Molly was all too well aware of the greater danger of him being beaten up by the three drunks he had dared to confront. She sped forward to interpose herself between the men and forced her assailant to deflect his punch in an attempt to avoid hitting her. Leandro still took a blow across one temple that sent him crashing to the floor. The back of his head banged off the tiled floor and for an instant there was blackness and he knew nothing. Time seemed to move seamlessly on, however, for when his eyes opened again he was staring up into instantly recognisable vibrant green as the waitress crouched over him, her anxiety obvious. She was close enough for the lemony scent of her curling hair and creamy skin to flare his nostrils and awaken a powerful sexual response.

When Molly collided with Leandro's honey dark gaze, it was as if the whole world ground to a halt and sent her spinning off into the unknown. Heat uncoiled in a lazy entangling loop in her pelvis and cut off her ability to breathe. Her body came alive in embarrassing places and throbbed as if a switch somewhere inside her had been flipped on.

The drunks cleared off and vanished into the gathering crowd when they realised how many people were watching the scene. Krystal Forfar waved away Molly with an angry gesture. 'I think you've caused enough trouble! Mr Carrera Marquez? Shall I call a doctor?'

Molly sprang upright and watched Leandro stagger slightly as he straightened while coolly denying the idea that he might require medical attention.

'I think you should go to hospital,' Molly volunteered unasked. 'You blacked out for a moment and you could have concussion.'

'Thank you, but I have sustained no injury,' Leandro drawled with arrogant assurance, smoothing down his rumpled jacket. 'I think I would like some fresh air, though. It's a little stuffy in here.'

'What the heck happened?' Brian demanded, hustling her away for a private chat.

Molly explained while Vanessa hovered.

'The Spanish guy is a real hero—just imagine the likes of him bothering to interfere because a drunk pinches your bum!' Vanessa exclaimed. 'It's not what you expect, is it?'

His behaviour had astonished Molly as well, but it had also impressed her, because the only other man she knew who would have intervened to stop a woman being harassed in that way was Jez. Molly took a plate over to the buffet and picked out a choice selection of the food and placed it on the tray with a drink. She carried it out through the French windows onto the balcony where Leandro Carrera Marquez had gone.

Lean bold profile taut, he was leaning on the parapet and looking out over the bright lights of the city.

'I wanted to thank you for telling that guy to lay off me. It was very brave,' Molly murmured in a rush as she set the tray down on the table behind him. 'I'm sorry you got thumped like that.'

'If you hadn't got in the way I would have hit him back,' Leandro traded, turning to look at her. He was still marvelling at the surge of rage that had gripped him when he'd seen the drunk touching her body. The sight of another man getting familiar with her had been deeply offensive to him.

'There were three of them and only one of you.' Molly stretched up on tiptoe to brush her fingertips very gently over the darkening bruise forming on his olive skin. 'You could have got really badly hurt and I feel guilty enough. I've brought you some food. Please eat something.'

The swell of her firm pointed breasts rubbed against his chest and her proximity gave him another opportunity to smell the already recognisable citrus-fresh scent of her hair. Raw sexual desire fired inside Leandro again with the force of a blowtorch. He studied the full soft curves of her generous pink mouth and burned to taste her. 'I'm not hungry for anything but you,' Leandro breathed thickly.

CHAPTER TWO

WHILE Molly looked up at him with vivid and curious green eyes, Leandro ditched all effort to resist temptation. He reached out and closed his arms round her to pull her into place against his lean powerful body.

Molly leant into him, her encouragement instinctive but new and strange enough to startle her. Long brown fingers meshed into her tumbling curls to tip up her face. She stretched up again and let her hands slide shyly through the silky depths of his springy hair. Her need to touch him was overpowering every inhibition. His wide, sensual mouth claimed hers with explosive passion.

Molly had never been kissed like that before, had never known such heat and urgency and excitement, and it was like being plunged into the eye of a storm. She felt dizzy and out of control. His tongue plunged between her lips and withdrew and quivering, scorching hunger pierced her like the blade of a knife. Elemental need leapt through her and screamed demands she was ill equipped to deal with. She trembled in sexual shock from the rush of sensation, her soft mouth still clinging to his as the peaks of her breasts tightened into taut, tingling buds. While her senses reeled from the touch and the taste of him her fingers closed into the edges of his jacket to hold onto him and keep herself steady.

A car alarm shrilled out somewhere in the street below and Leandro tensed and jerked his dark head up, his thoughts diving into a free fall of shock as he recognised that he was acting on impulse and without his usual intelligent restraint. Yet, letting go of her slight figure which seemed to fit so very neatly to his more solid masculine frame was one of the hardest things he had ever had to make himself do for he was painfully aroused.

'I'm sorry,' he murmured, and it was a mental challenge for him even to come up with the right phrase in English.

Molly was in a daze as well and quite unable to muster rational thought. 'Why? *Sorry?*' she queried as his lean hands closed over her narrow shoulders and set her very deliberately back from him.

Molly blinked, watching him curve a hand round the balcony's ornate ironwork balustrade until his knuckles showed white with tension below his brown skin. He had beautifully shaped hands with long, elegant fingers. The steady beat of music and the pound of feet on the dance floor travelled out from the wedding party inside the house. Her attention roved up to his strong jaw line, straight classic nose and stunning profile. She wasn't surprised that she couldn't take her eyes off him: he had the sleek, dark, sinful beauty of a fallen angel. But what had she been playing at? Letting one of the guests kiss her when she was supposed to be working? Was she crazy? Her job was all that stood between her and unemployment. She had been there once and didn't want to undergo that humiliation and stress again.

'It shouldn't have happened and normally it wouldn't

have,' Leandro breathed, finally opting to acknowledge the strange restless mood that had afflicted him for the past week.

Molly recalled the fact that he had virtually pushed *her* away and a shamed flush swept across her face as high as her hairline. No, that embrace shouldn't have happened and it said nothing in her favour that he had been the first of them to register that truth and act on it. Where had her wits been? But she still felt hot and shivery and awesomely aware of him. The lure of the excitement he had generated was potent and her body was cooling into a state of taut disappointment. The hot colour in her cheeks refused to disperse.

'I'm not quite myself. Perhaps I've had too much to drink. What other explanation could there be for my behaviour?' Leandro demanded with chilling cool, noting the way her complexion had coloured and wondering what age she was, for at that moment she looked very young to him. '*Dios mio!* You are the waitress.'

In receipt of that blunt rejection of who and what she was, Molly turned very pale. She was a person, an individual, another human being before she was a waitress, she thought painfully. 'I should have realised that you'd be an out-and-out snob. Don't worry. You don't need to make excuses. I'm not naïve enough to think a kiss meant there was a relationship in the offing and you're not my type anyway!'

In a series of brisk, no-nonsense movements, Molly cleared the tray on the table and headed back indoors.

'You're gorgeous, *querida*,' Leandro heard himself murmur huskily. 'I didn't need any other excuse.'

Her colour fluctuated at that unexpected compliment as she walked away. Gorgeous? Since when had she been gorgeous? She had been called pretty once or twice when she was all done up, but there was no truth whatsoever in the label he had just given her. She was five feet one inch and she had a mane of black curls that was often impossible to control. Her skin was good and she considered herself lucky in that she could pretty much eat what she liked without gaining weight. Those were her only advantages in her own estimation.

'Were you outside with Mr Carrera Marquez?' the bride's mother demanded angrily, planting herself combatively in Molly's path. 'Why did you go out there to bother him?'

'I wasn't bothering him. I needed to thank him for intervening with those men on my behalf and I took him some food.' Molly lifted her chin at a defiant angle.

The tall blonde woman stared down at her with angry superiority. 'I've already told your manager that I won't have you working in my home again. You've got the wrong attitude,' she censured curtly. 'You had no business making a personal approach to one of our guests and spoiling my daughter's wedding.'

That unjust rebuke made Molly's eyes prickle with angry tears and she had to bite back a sharp retaliation. She had done nothing wrong. She had been insulted verbally and physically, but nobody was about to say sorry to a mere waitress. She went back into the kitchen where Brian suggested she start helping the chef to clean up. She worked steadily and fast. The evening wore on until the chatter of the guests slowly died down along with the music and people left to go home.

'Do another check out there for glasses,' Brian instructed.

Molly took out a tray and the first person she saw

was the Spanish banker, leaning up against a wall at an elegant angle and talking into his mobile phone. He was ordering a taxi. She refused even to look in his direction as she hurried through to the next room to pick up a collection of abandoned glasses. The whole time she was within view, Leandro watched her small figure like a hawk.

She had said he wasn't her type but he was convinced that that had been pure bravado. Yet she was definitely not the sort of woman he had gone for in the past. Tall, elegant blondes like Aloise had always been Leandro's style. But Molly got to him on a much more basic plane. The sensual sway of her curvaceous hips would have attracted any red-blooded male's attention, Leandro told himself grimly. The wild mop of black curls anchored on top of her small head, the huge green eyes and the gloriously full inviting mouth were drop-dead sexy attributes before he even glanced below her chin. Just looking at her, he got hot and hard. Remembering the soft allure of her mouth opening for him and the eagerness of her response did nothing to improve his condition. He needed a cold shower. He needed *a woman*, he acknowledged, his wide mouth compressing into a line, for he was furious that he could have so little control over his own body.

The rooms were almost empty by the time Molly had finished helping to load the catering van. Putting on her coat, she walked back round to the front of the house on her way to where she had parked her car. It was a surprise to find the Spanish banker standing out on the pavement. It was a freezing cold wintry night and he had no coat on over his suit. Wind was whistling down the street and he looked chilled to the marrow.

'Didn't your taxi come yet?' she asked before she could think better of taking notice of him.

'Apparently they're very busy tonight. I don't think I have ever been so cold in my life. How do you bear this climate?' Leandro enquired between gritted white teeth.

'Choice didn't come into it.' Molly thought what a miserable evening he had had and sympathy softened her stiff stance and expression. 'Look, I would offer you a lift home but I don't want to give you the wrong idea—'

'How would I get the wrong idea?' Leandro cut in, knowing it was going to be a very long time, if ever, before he went out again without his chauffeur and limousine to transport him around. It had not occurred to him until it was too late that he could not possibly drive himself home when he had had several drinks.

Molly tilted her chin, luminous green eyes proffering a challenge. 'I'm not stalking you or in any way expressing a personal interest in you,' she spelt out with scrupulous care.

Leandro studied her with sudden intense amusement because what was in his mind was the exact opposite—he was thinking that if he just let her walk away he would never see her again. *Never.* There was just one problem: Leandro was discovering that he was not prepared to accept that eventuality. 'I know you're not stalking me. I'll take a lift,' he murmured softly.

'I'll get my car.' Having crossed the road, Molly went round the corner and unlocked and climbed into her ancient Mini. She was already asking herself what had come over her, why she hadn't just walked on past and left him to freeze. She hadn't even asked where he lived and suspected that it would most probably be well out of her way.

The appearance of the vibrant pink car initially took Leandro aback. It was as quirky and full of personality as he suspected its owner was. He attempted to get in, realised that he had to shift the seat back to accommodate his long legs and did so before folding his lean, powerful length into the tight space. 'You like pink,' he remarked.

'It's an easy colour to spot in a car park. Where do you live?'

His address was as exclusive and expensive as she believed he was, but it was comparatively close to the part of town they were in. 'How did you get to the exhibition tonight?' she prompted.

'By car, but I've drunk too much to drive,' Leandro stated.

'Is that why you said you weren't yourself earlier?' Molly queried, shooting him a curious look as she stopped at a set of traffic lights. He turned his handsome dark head to look at her and she marvelled at the hot gold colour his dark brooding eyes acquired in stronger light.

'No. Today was the anniversary of my wife's death a year ago. I've been unsettled all week,' Leandro imparted, and immediately wondered why he was admitting something so personal to her, since it was not at all like him.

For a split second, Molly froze, and then her natural warmth and sympathy took charge of her response. She reached across and squeezed his hand. 'I'm so sorry,' she said sincerely. 'Was she ill?'

Startled by that affectionate gesture of support,

Leandro had stiffened. 'No, she crashed her car. My fault. We had an…exchange of words before she went out,' he said tautly.

An exchange of words? Did he mean they'd had a row? 'Of course it wasn't your fault,' Molly told him with firm conviction. 'You shouldn't be blaming yourself. Unless you were physically behind the wheel, it was a tragic accident and it's not healthy to think of it any other way.'

Her outspoken candour and practicality were a refreshing change when compared to the majority of people, who carefully avoided making any reference to the thorny subject of Aloise's sudden death. Perhaps it was true that it was easier to talk to strangers, Leandro mused reflectively, for he was unable to recall any other occasion when he had spontaneously abandoned his reserve to confide in anyone else.

He was a widower, Molly thought ruefully. She didn't know how she felt about that, only that it was an unexpected fact. 'You feel guilty about kissing me as well, don't you?' she guessed.

His classic bronzed profile went rigid at that reminder. She had hit a bullseye. Suddenly her candour was unwelcome and gauche in the extreme. 'I don't think we need to discuss that,' he drawled in a tone of finality.

Molly changed gear and her knuckles accidentally skimmed a length of lean muscular thigh as she did so. 'Sorry,' she muttered uncomfortably. 'There isn't much space in this car.'

The atmosphere was tense.

'How long have you worked as a waitress?' Leandro asked, gracefully negotiating a passage through the awkward silence that had fallen.

'I started out as a part-timer when I was at art college. My earnings helped to keep my student loans under control,' Molly told him. 'I'm a potter when I can afford to be, but waitressing is what it takes to pay my bills.'

Silence fell again. She parked near the strikingly modern apartment building he pointed out. He thanked her and tried to get out but the door wouldn't open. The faulty handle, which she had thought was fixed, was acting up again. With a muffled apology, Molly got out and hurried round the bonnet to open the passenger door from the outside.

Leandro climbed out and straightened, relieved to be escaping the cramped restrictions of the car interior. Molly, he noticed, barely reached the middle of his chest. There was something intensely feminine about her slight build and diminutive stature. He had a sudden explosively sexual image of lifting her up against him and only with the greatest difficulty did he manage to shut it out. Even so, his body reacted with instant enthusiasm. He wanted to pull her into his arms, seal her lush body to his and make love to her. He was stunned by the amount of restraint it took to keep his hands off her and furious that he couldn't keep his libido under better control.

With a swift goodbye, Molly hurried back round the car and jumped in. She watched him stride across the road and enter the well-lit foyer of the block. She got a last glimpse of his lean, darkly handsome face as he exchanged a greeting with the porter on the desk before turning away and moving out of view. She felt horribly let down, shockingly disappointed that he was gone.

Shaking her head at her own foolishness, she was clasping her seat belt, when she noticed something lying on the floor. Undoing the belt she bent down and stretched out a hand to scoop up the item. It was a man's wallet and it could only belong to the man who had just vacated her car. With an impatient groan, she undid her belt and climbed out again.

The porter had no problem in identifying whom she was talking about and he offered to deliver the wallet. But Molly preferred to return the item in person. The porter tried to phone Leandro's apartment but when there was no answer he advised Molly to go on up to the top floor in the lift. While it whirred upwards, she asked herself what she was playing at. Here she was literally chasing after him. Perhaps she should have let the porter return the wallet. Had she secretly wanted an excuse to see Leandro again? Her face was burning with colour at that suspicion when the lift doors whirred back with an electronic clunk. She stepped out into a snazzy semi-circular hall. The Spaniard was standing in front of the only door going through his pockets. He wheeled round at the sound of the lift. His winged ebony brows lifted in surprise at the sight of her.

'Is this what you're looking for?' Molly held out the wallet. 'I found it lying on the floor of my car.'

'Exactly what I'm looking for.' He flipped open the wallet to extract a card and opened the door straightaway. 'Thank you…no, don't leave.' He strode back to her to prevent her from walking back into the lift. 'Join me for a drink.'

'No, I can't. That's not why I came up here,' Molly protested, her discomfiture unhidden.

'But it should have been, *querida*.' Intent dark golden eyes glittered down into hers. 'Why are we both trying to walk away from this?'

And Molly didn't need to ask him what 'this' encompassed because she already knew. From the minute she saw him her every thought had contained him and even then it had required effort not to just stand still and stare at him while she memorised every tiny facet of his appearance for future recall and enjoyment. The thought that she might never see him again upset her even though she didn't know him. She was as drawn to him as an iron filing to a magnet and her brain had nothing to do with the terrifyingly powerful hold of that attraction.

'Because it's crazy!' Molly exclaimed jerkily, backing away a step as if she was trying to steel herself back into departure mode again.

Leandro closed a lean hand round her narrow-boned wrist and urged her into his apartment. 'I don't want to stand out here talking. Our every move is being recorded by security cameras,' he explained.

He flipped on lights to reveal a large hall with a marble floor and a fashionable glass table bearing a bronze sculpture. It looked like a picture out of a glossy interior design magazine and it unnerved her. 'Look at the way you live!' Molly shifted an uneasy hand in a demonstrative gesture. 'You're a banker. I'm a waitress. We might as well be aliens from different planets.'

'Maybe that novelty is part of the attraction and why not?' Leandro fielded, moving slowly forward to close both hands round her fragile wrists to maintain a physical connection with her. 'I don't want you to leave…'

The pads of his thumbs rubbed gently at the delicate blue-veined skin of her inner wrist. She looked up at him and knew it to be a fatal act, for when she met those stunning dark eyes she could hardly think straight, never mind breathe. Although she didn't want to leave, she almost never took risks of any kind. Life had taught her that the costs of being anything other than sensible and cautious were likely to be high and painful.

'Feeling like this terrifies me,' she confessed in a whisper.

'You make me feel more alive than I have felt in more years than I care to recall, *querida*.' His brooding gaze was welded to her while he momentarily fought to comprehend the intensity of his desire for her. 'That's not scary, that's cause for celebration.'

It shook her that he was describing exactly what she was feeling as well. Somehow it seemed to make her reaction to him more acceptable and she shut out the misgivings striving to be heard in the back of her mind. Even as she looked back at him sensual energy was leaping and dancing through her small, taut frame, tightening the tender peaks of her breasts into taut buds and spilling heat between her thighs in a storm of powerful physical responses that turned her bones to water and her brain to mush. With a stifled imprecation, Leandro bent down and drove her pink lips apart in a demanding kiss.

Molly gasped. His urgency was exactly what her trembling, eager body craved. She felt him peel off her coat. She was locked to the muscular strength of his lithe powerful physique, her breasts crushed against his hard chest, her lips parting in welcome to the erotic plunge of his tongue in her mouth.

In receipt of her response, Leandro shuddered, sinking his hands to her hips in the fitted skirt and hauling her bodily up against him. She locked her hands round his neck and kissed him back with breathless fervour.

'Do you want a drink?' he asked her.

'Not if it means you'll stop kissing me,' Molly told him, small fingers delving into his luxuriant black hair to hold him to her. She had the same sense of wonder she experienced when she created a new design on her potter's wheel, that same heady glorious conviction that what she was doing was eerily exactly right.

'I *can't* stop,' Leandro groaned, trailing his lips down her slender neck in a series of darting, rousing kisses that made her squirm and whimper as he discovered newly erogenous zones of skin. Her unconcealed enthusiasm only added to his pleasure in her. His tongue flicked the sensitive roof of her mouth and she shivered violently. 'Stay with me tonight,' he urged.

At first surprise and dismay gripped her and then her agile brain pulled free of sensual lockdown for long enough to reason that invitation out. They weren't teenagers kissing on a doorstep. She might be a good deal less experienced than many a teenager, but she was a grown woman and he was very definitely an adult male. What happened next was entirely her decision. She thought about letting go of him, saying goodnight, probably never seeing him again. Her skin chilled and her insides turned hollow and cold at that threat. Her arms tightened round him. She wanted to lock him up and keep the key to his captivity safely attached to a chain round her throat. She had never felt that way before about a man and she wasn't at all sure she liked it.

'But I'm a waitress,' she reminded him shakily.

'It doesn't matter. It truly doesn't matter, *mi muñeca*,' Leandro asserted in a driven undertone. 'What matters is who you are when you're with me.'

She looked up and was ensnared by a smile that made

her heart pound and rocked her world like an earthquake. Suddenly being sensible and careful had zero attraction. He made her want to be daring and the sort of female who inspired men to acts of madness. 'I'll stay—'

His arms tightened round her and the hungry ravishment of his mouth on hers left her in no doubt of his reaction to her agreement. She felt the rigid heat of his erection against her and she trembled, both intimidated and excited by the effect she had on him. He was so much a man, so male in comparison to the youths she was accustomed to. He carried her out of the hall into a room lit by moonlight. He sank down on the wide bed and lowered her to her feet between his spread thighs.

'Now you're at my level it will be much easier to kiss you,' he pointed out thickly, reaching up to unclip her hair and using his hands to brush the lush mane of blue-black curls back from her brow and guide the tumbling mass down over her slight shoulders. 'You have the most beautiful hair.'

'Far too much of it and it's horribly curly,' she told him helplessly.

'Not for me, *querida.*' Leandro ran slow possessive hands over her, his thumbs brushing the protuberant nipples that were visible through her thin cotton blouse, his palms smoothing over the full curve of her hips below her tiny waist. 'You also have the most wonderful shape.'

The hungry heat burning through Molly was reaching a boiling point of impatience. She leant forward and brushed her soft pink lips over his in an experimental fashion while she yanked his silk tie loose, slipped the knot and cast it aside. Her breath fanned a smooth bronzed cheekbone as she gazed into eyes that were dark as ebony in the moonlight and unfathomable. 'I hope you're not going to be a mistake,' she muttered anxiously, conscious that she was taking a chance on him by throwing caution to the four winds.

Having shed his jacket, Leandro hauled her back to him and kissed her with passionate, probing force until she was breathless. 'Nothing that feels this good could possibly be a mistake,' he declared.

She wondered if he would feel the same way in the morning, wondered how she would feel as well, but while his skilful hands were moving over her, sending her every pulse and skin cell crazy with wild hunger, she found it impossible to second guess the future. He unzipped her skirt and pushed it down, lifting her out of it and just as quickly unbuttoning her shirt and extracting her from it. The ease with which he undressed her suggested a level of sophistication that made her nervous. Her breasts spilled from the cups of her bra and he moulded the soft, pouting mounds with a masculine growl of appreciation. His fingers teased her swollen pink nipples and he cradled her across his thighs to let his sensual mouth and tongue play with the delicate straining buds.

So much unfamiliar sensation engulfed Molly that a stifled sob of response was dredged from her. The power of what she was feeling was overwhelming. Her skin was damp with perspiration, her heart thumping like a road drill while an ache of longing close to actual pain throbbed between her slender legs. She was desperate to touch him as well, but he didn't give her the chance. He laid her down on the bed and got up again to undress.

CHAPTER THREE

DRY-MOUTHED, Molly watched as Leandro stripped. She had sketched nude models in life class at college, so the masculine anatomy was far from being a complete mystery to her. But she had never seen a male body that could aspire to the sheer magnificence of Leandro's sleek bronzed physique. He was superbly built from his muscular chest to his hard flat stomach and long, powerful thighs.

He was also fiercely erect. Her rapt gaze widened slightly and red stained her cheeks, for there was a good deal more of him in that department than she had expected, a discovery that sent a mortifying stab of virginal uncertainty through her slight frame. For the first time she wished she were a little more practised. Unconcerned by his nakedness and silvered by moonlight, he strolled fluidly back to the bed to join her. Her palms smoothed over his strong pectoral muscles. He felt like warm, hair-roughened bronze, the pelt of black curls on his chest arrowing down into an intriguing line over his belly.

'Show me that you want me,' Leandro growled.

Emboldened by that request, she dipped her hands to

touch him with greater intimacy. She traced and stroked the iron-hard length of his sex, fascinated by his alien masculinity and encouraged by his low-pitched sounds of pleasure.

But it wasn't long before he made her desist and gathered her into his arms again. 'I can't take much of that, *querida*,' he confessed, plunging his mouth down on a succulent nipple as lush as pink velvet, dividing his attention between it and its equally responsive twin while his fingers finally delved into the hot, moist, tender core of her.

In the first moments of that erotic exploration, Molly thought she would not be able to bear anything at all. Her body instantly felt like a fire raging out of her control. Ripples of lascivious wanton pleasure enveloped her from the first expert invasion of his fingers. He found the tiny bud that controlled her response and lingered there with devastating effect. Her breath rasped raw in her throat and she whimpered beneath that sensual torment of sensation. She couldn't speak for excitement. Her body twisted and jerked like a puppet in the hold of a tyrannical master. There was a tight, tormenting ball of need swelling in her loins and pushing her to an agonising pitch of hunger.

'I can't wait any longer,' Leandro confessed, coming over her and pinning her hands to the bed beneath his while he slid between her thighs. His brilliant eyes smouldered pure gold as he stared down at her. He had never wanted anything or anybody as much as he wanted her at that moment. He had never known such a high of sexual intensity. With her raven hair spread across his pillows, her crystalline green eyes shimmering and her voluptuous mouth swollen from the onslaught of his, he thought she was irresistible.

Molly cried out as he drove into her resisting flesh with one urgent thrust. His power was too potent to be denied and he forged a bold passage into her honeyed depths, stretching and filling her to capacity.

'I hurt you!' Leandro exclaimed and stilled.

'No, it doesn't matter!' Molly protested, for she was embarrassed and the discomfort was already ebbing as her receptive body slowly adjusted to him. He felt amazing inside her and a rising tide of heat consumed her again. 'Don't stop.'

Leandro was astonished by what her behaviour in combination with her body was telling him. His ebony brows drew together in a questioning frown. '*Dios mio!* Are you a virgin?'

'*Was*,' Molly countered awkwardly, keen not to discuss the matter just at that moment.

His lean, darkly handsome face was taut. 'You should have warned me, *mi gatita.*'

'It felt too private to mention,' Molly admitted uncomfortably.

Leandro dealt her an incredulous look and then he flung back his proud dark head and laughed with rich appreciation. 'You make me smile.' He dropped a teasing kiss on her bemused brow and shifted his lean hips, reacquainting her with his presence until she gasped in shaken response.

The hot, hungry heat burned inside her again, her body eagerly quickening to the sexual dominance of his. He sank deep into her and withdrew again and repeated that torturous cycle again and again until she was shaking and arching beneath him, almost driven out of her mind by the urgent desire he had ignited. Nothing mattered but the satisfaction she was reaching for and the delirious excitement of the pace he set. Tiny feverish tremors passed through her. She moved against him, caught up in the intensity of her hunger. When she reached orgasm, it was as if the whole world stopped and flung her sky-high. Waves of exquisite pleasure gripped her and she writhed under him in an ecstasy of abandon. In the throes of the same satisfaction, he shuddered and drove deep and she lifted her hips to receive him and held him close in the aftermath.

Afterwards she was in a state of sleepy wonderment at what she had just learned about her own body's amazing capacity for enjoyment. She wanted to stay awake because she had never before felt so close to another human being and she loved that sense of intimacy, but she had also never felt so tired in her life. He kissed her and he muttered some Spanish stuff.

'I don't speak the lingo,' she mumbled sleepily.

'I'm too tired to speak English.'

'So shut up and go to sleep,' Molly countered, snuggling up to him and closing a possessive arm round him.

In the moonlight, Leandro elevated an ebony brow and turned her over so that she was lying on her side. A mark at the base of her spine caught his attention. A scar? His finger traced the tattoo of hot-pink lips. He pushed back the sheet and saw another illustration on her ankle. It was of a tiny trail of silvery blue stars. He smiled, covered her up again and tugged her back against him. She was totally different from any other woman he had ever met or bedded. Definitely not Duquesa material—but the perfect candidate for the role of mistress.

Why not? In bed she was pure enticement and as hot

for him as he was for her. He had a very healthy sex drive and too many years had passed since he was able to give his libido a free rein. The idea of having relaxation time with a warm, willing woman like Molly at the end of a long stressful day at the bank was immensely appealing. He enjoyed the fact that she talked to him on a level as if he were an ordinary person. She was comfortable and confident within herself. He couldn't ever remember a woman telling him to shut up before—even as a joke. She was novel, she was fresh and he was bored and determined to break free of the web of duty and responsibility that entrapped him. Just for once, Leandro mused, he was going to do exactly what he wanted to do and to hell with the consequences!

Wakening, Molly lifted her lashes and registered that she was lying in a strange bed in an equally strange room. It was still dark but the dawn was lighting up the distant horizon. The décor had a cool art deco style and the room was really large. Only someone very rich could afford that amount of space and that kind of furniture in a city as expensive as London. The events of the previous night flooded back to her and she went rigid. She had slept with Leandro and she couldn't even pronounce, never mind spell, his surname. As she sneaked a leg towards the edge of the bed to get up a long masculine arm closed round her and drew her back.

'Don't even think about leaving, *querida*,' Leandro husked, his breath stirring her hair. 'It's only seven.'

'This is really embarrassing,' Molly mumbled. 'I don't even have a toothbrush with me.'

Leandro worked hard at not laughing at that inept admission. 'I have a spare. I'll order breakfast. I have something I would very much like to discuss with you.'

All Molly wanted just then was a magic wand to wave that would whisk her from being naked in his bed back to the sanctuary of her own bedroom. Her clothes were scattered on the polished wood floor. I'm a slut, she thought wretchedly, a total slut.

Leandro was talking on the bedside phone in Spanish at a great rate. He sounded like someone accustomed to rapping out instructions. But what did she know about him? He was amazingly good-looking? Chivalrous towards humble waitresses? Fantastic in bed? Averse to the cold? A widower? Well, these days that last fact did tell her something about his character, she reasoned. He had been prepared to commit to a future with someone and had got married at a reasonably early age, which was unusual.

'I'll use the bathroom next door,' he told her lazily.

To his list of attributes, Molly added a plus for tact. Without turning her head, however, she waited until she heard the door snap shut on his departure before she scrambled out of bed, gathered up the clothes she had been wearing the night before and raced into the en-suite bathroom clutching them.

Her curls looked as though she had stuck a finger in an electric socket. She groaned out loud and rifled the drawers of the vanity unit for the toothbrush she had been promised. The corner shower was digitally operated so she couldn't work out how to use it and made do with washing at the sink as best she could. As she dressed she was conscious that her body ached even worse than it had after the charity mini-marathon she had done with Jez the previous year.

She had a dim erotic memory of wakening during the night and making love with Leandro again. She had made the approach, which had resulted in his long, achingly slow and spellbinding seduction that had made her cry out his name at the top of her voice. She cringed at the recollection of her audacity while she fiddled with her hair, struggling to tame her wild curls into some semblance of order without the aid of her usual weapons. Only when she no longer had any excuse to linger did she emerge from the bedroom. She only knew one thing: had she had the chance to go back to the previous night she would still have chosen to stay with him and experience what had followed.

The dining room enjoyed a stunning view of the Thames. A waiter was there presiding over a trolley stacked with a wide selection of food and Molly was astonished by the concept of anyone buying in breakfast for two complete with service. But her wide eyes still swivelled straight across to Leandro, who was poised by the window. He commanded the scene, sheathed in a superbly tailored black pinstripe suit that was the very epitome of banking chic. He looked sinfully beautiful but cool and remote. Her tummy gave an uneasy lurch as if she were under threat. She didn't know how to behave or what to say to him.

With an authoritative nod, Leandro told the waiter he could leave because they would serve themselves. Her face flushed as she carefully avoided a direct meeting with his thickly lashed dark eyes, Molly wiped damp palms down the sides of her fitted black skirt. It was obvious to her that ordering people around came very naturally indeed to Leandro. She had never been more conscious of her lowly status than when she was standing there still garbed in her work clothes while he summarily dismissed the waiter from his duties.

Conscious her tummy was rumbling, she lifted a small box of cereal and put it in a bowl before taking a seat. The apartment was even more opulent than she had initially appreciated and she felt more like a fish out of water than ever.

'Last night…' Leandro hesitated, searching for the right words with which to outline his offer as he helped himself to fresh fruit. 'It was fantastic.'

'Hmm.' Molly nodded, her mouth too full to speak and even if it hadn't been she had no idea what she might have replied to that surprisingly intimate comment. Clothed and in daylight, Leandro was horrendously intimidating. She could barely credit that she had spent the night in his arms.

Leandro breathed in deep. 'In fact it was so incredible that I want to hang onto you, *querida*.'

Molly almost choked on her cereal. 'Hang *onto* me?' she parroted without comprehension.

'I lead a very busy existence in which I rarely have time to lighten up, which is one very good reason why I would like you to become a part of my life. I like your cheerful attitude and I need to relax more,' Leandro imparted levelly. 'We both have something that the other needs. It would be an exchange of mutual benefit. You would enjoy the financial security to indulge your ambition to be an artisan potter and I would be happy to make that possible.'

Her smooth brow had indented and her almond-shaped eyes were bright with bewilderment. 'What on earth are you trying to say?'

'That I would be prepared to buy you somewhere suitable to live and money need no longer be a source of concern for you,' Leandro spelt out softly. 'No more waitressing—I would cover all your expenses. It would be my pleasure to do so.'

Molly studied him fixedly, her heartbeat thumping so fast and loud that it felt as if it were trapped in her tight throat. 'Why would you offer to buy me somewhere to live? Why would you want to pay my bills? Exactly what kind of a relationship are you offering me?'

'I want you to be my mistress and stay in my life, *querida*. In the background of my life rather than the forefront of it, it is true,' Leandro conceded, belatedly wondering whether she was capable of being discreet. 'But you would still be important to me.'

As he quantified his objective, Molly had turned pale and then suddenly colour ran up like a banner beneath her creamy skin and burnished it to hot pink. Anger strongly laced with outrage left her light-headed and threatened to erupt from her like a volcano. Her jewelled eyes fiery with disbelief, she rammed her hands down flat on the table top and pushed herself upright. 'You arrogant, condescending rat!' she launched at him furiously. 'Your *mistress*? What was last night supposed to be? A trial run for the position? You have no business even suggesting such a thing to me!'

'You don't need to use abuse to make your point,' Leandro censured with freezing cool. 'In my world such arrangements between men and women are common and accepted.'

'Not in mine!' Molly gasped, stricken by the awareness that if he had just asked to see her again she would have snatched at the opportunity. Instead he had put an offensive commercial price on any future relationship and made it very clear that she wasn't good enough to occupy any more equal or public role in his life. That clear fact hurt like a knife twisting inside her, echoing as it did the painful rejections she had had to deal with throughout her life. *Not good enough.* Sometimes it seemed to Molly that she was never good enough for anything she really wanted.

Leandro, his lean, strong face impassive, continued to study her with a detachment that chilled Molly to the marrow. 'You can't be that naive.'

Leandro had never been with a woman who didn't want to profit from being with him in some way. Even as a teenager he had been the target of elaborate female stratagems designed to attract his interest and entrap him. Fabulous wealth was a very powerful draw. He had learned young that sex was invariably offered in the expectation that the act of sharing his bed would be rewarded with frequent bouts of financial generosity. And then there were the women who didn't primarily want his money, but who had their social ambitions squarely set on marrying him and using his ancient name and aristocratic lineage to gain an entry to the most exclusive and privileged stratum of Spanish society.

'Listen to me—I don't need anyone but myself to make my dreams come true,' Molly told him half an octave higher. 'I certainly don't need any man to keep me and I *never* will! I manage fine on my own—'

'You're capable of being more than a waitress,' Leandro contended grimly.

'And a great deal more than being your mistress too!' Molly launched back at him in heated challenge. 'However low I may sink in life, you can be sure that

I'll never be desperate enough to surrender my self-respect and sell myself to you for sex!'

'Shorn of melodrama, was that a no?' Leandro surveyed her with level dark as midnight eyes, his lean, powerful face tight with reserve and cool. Displeasure radiated from him like a force field but his self-control, unlike hers, was absolute.

'Yes, that was a *no*, and now I think it's time I cleared off and went home.' Her voice sounded choky and tears were stinging the backs of her eyes. 'How could you belittle me with a sleazy offer like that? I'm not interested in being some dirty little secret in your life!'

'It wouldn't be like that between us. I only want to keep you close—'

'But only in the most demeaning way!' Molly cut in with biting scorn. 'Not as an equal. You wear your belief in your superiority like a medal, don't you? But I'm not some little toy you can buy to entertain yourself in your free time and where do you get off suggesting that I am?'

Affronted by her sustained verbal attack, Leandro unfolded from his seat to his full imposing height and viewed her with sardonic eyes. 'You were happy enough to be with me last night. Did I treat you like a toy?'

Molly's cheeks burned hotter than fire, as she suspected that she had been more guilty of treating him like the ultimate adult woman's plaything the night before, for she had fully satisfied all her curiosity. 'Last night was last night. I didn't know what was on your mind then. I liked you until we had this conversation—'

A black brow quirked. 'Did you? I would have said that you wanted me the same way I wanted—and *still* want—you. Can you really switch off like that?'

Taut as a bow string, she stared back at him, knowing that it would not be so easy to switch off her responses or forget that overwhelming passion that had proved so very addictive. His stunning eyes rested on her, cool and unreadable. 'Yes,' she lied curtly. 'Yes, I can. I'm not a forgiving person, either!'

Molly stalked out to the hall where she had seen her coat lying across a chair. She had only snatched it up when it was removed from her grasp and politely extended for her to slip into by Leandro.

'You really put the "o" into offensive with your offers, but, hey, you've got exquisite manners!' Molly sniped as she dug her arms into the sleeves and spun back round to face him.

Leandro nudged her coat out of his path and slid a business card into the front pocket of her white blouse. 'My private phone number. For the moment when you come to appreciate what you're passing up.'

'That moment will never come—I'm making a lucky escape from a guy who belongs in the Dark Ages and still thinks it's all right to treat women like sex objects!' she hissed back.

Leandro curved lean fingers to her cheekbones to hold her steady and plundered her soft pink lips in a smoulderingly sexual kiss that lit a fire in her pelvis and made her tremble. 'You'll come running back—you won't be able to help yourself, *mi gatita*,' he forecast huskily. 'I won't let you go. That's a promise.'

He didn't have her phone number, he didn't even know where she lived, so Molly wasn't too concerned by that macho assurance, which set her teeth on edge. She walked into the lift with an oddly bereft feeling dogging her mood. She refused to acknowledge it and her thoughts were soon turned to much more practical matters when she discovered that her car had acquired a parking ticket since she had left it the evening before. Such penalties were incredibly expensive and she was, as always, broke. With a grimace of annoyance, she drove off.

Leandro called his security team to ensure that she was followed. There was no way he was letting her go again. The more she fought, the more he wanted her for he now recognised her absolute uniqueness. She wasn't after his money or his social pedigree, but she did *want* him very much. Purely as a man. He had no doubt whatsoever on that score. Indeed a hard slanting smile of amused satisfaction banished the grim cast of his handsome mouth. He remembered her in his bed last night. She had carefully nudged him awake, her Cupid's-bow mouth soft and coaxing and pure dynamite on his shoulder and his chest before travelling to more sensitive places as she became ever more enterprising. He recalled her helpless giggles when she got it wrong and the white hot glory of pleasure engulfing him when he showed her how to get it right. No way was he letting her walk away from him now. In the most basic terms and on a level that appealed to his every atavistic masculine fibre, she was *his* discovery and *his* creation.

It was only when she was gone and he was striding out to his limousine to head for the bank that Leandro stilled and realised in shock that the night before he had been guilty of a glaring oversight. He had not used condoms with her and, bearing in mind her lack of experience, it was unlikely that she was taking any contraceptive precautions on her own behalf. He swore soft and low in Spanish, stunned by his omission. Although, given

the five childless years of his marriage, it was a challenge
for him to believe that there could be a genuine risk of
her falling pregnant by him…

CHAPTER FOUR

IN THE act of trying to listen to a long involved speech from one of the bank's most senior directors, Leandro drifted into an erotic daydream.

As the self-justifying speech went on and endlessly on Leandro added elaborate layer on layer to the fantasy. He pictured Molly spreadeagled naked in the golden glow of the hot Spanish sunshine, her lush white breasts crowned by straining pink peaks that glistened damply with the champagne he was licking from her voluptuous curves. He was remembering the tantalising glide of her hair across his stomach and the velvet soft glory of her mouth…

'Mr Carrera Marquez?'

Leandro pulled instantaneously free of the seductive images that had captured an imagination he had not known he possessed. Even though his body was hot and heavy with discomfort and sexual need was a tormenting pulse-beat through his big powerful frame, he snapped straight back into cut-throat business mode.

'My opinion? In a nutshell? Get tough. Don't accept excuses for poor performance. Sack the management team. They've had their chance and blown it. Give that opportunity to hungrier employees,' Leandro advised without hesitation, and he brought the meeting to a close with the cool, economic efficiency that had made him a living legend in financial circles.

Closely followed by his phalanx of aides, his handsome dark head held high, Leandro strode down the corridor. He was incensed by the erotic recollections that had recently dared to cloud his concentration at inappropriate moments during his working day. But had sex ever been that good for him before? That wild? That hot? If it had been, he couldn't recall it. Possibly he had waited too long to ease the natural needs of his body and now all the pent-up hunger of a year's celibacy was tormenting him for release.

To that end, he finally made use of one of the many phone numbers he had had pressed on him since Aloise's death. He dined out with a beautiful blonde divorcee who had thrown herself at him previously with an enthusiasm that any sex-starved male should have revelled in. Unhappily, Leandro discovered that his seething libido was stubbornly impervious to the blonde's attractions. He still wanted Molly and it seemed that no other woman would do.

But why make a production out of that fact? Leandro asked himself with the equivalent of a mental shrug. He had had a lot of women in his life before he married and now that settled phase was well and truly over. Life was short. Sex was just sex and he was young and healthy. He worked hard, why shouldn't he play hard as well? There was nothing wrong with the pursuit of pleasure. Furthermore he had the perfect excuse for seeking out Molly again: he had to check that their night together had had no lasting repercussions.

* * *

Molly vented her exasperation with a groan of frustration when she removed her pots from the electric kiln in the shed. Several pieces had stuck to the trivet because she had been too liberal with the glaze. Under pressure from her, those items cracked. More unnecessary breakages! In recent days she had made more than her fair share of costly mistakes while she'd worked.

But then her emotions were eating her up because she was still so angry with herself for sleeping with Leandro, Molly acknowledged ruefully. Meeting Leandro and falling victim to his charms had forced her to accept that she had more in common with her birth mother, Cathy, than she had ever wanted to know. Cathy had been very prone to following casual impulses with men she'd never taken the time to get to know and she had called those urges, 'love', and their fulfilment, 'spontaneity'.

In comparison, Molly was less kind with her labels and over the past week and a half she had at various times called herself terminally stupid, reckless and naive. Leandro's attitude to her the morning after had been the ultimate put-down and had set the seal on her humiliation. She had given her body to a guy who wanted a tame woman to lock in a custom-built cage for his sexual gratification. He had neither respected nor appreciated her. How much lower could she have sunk?

She was in the kitchen making coffee when the front doorbell went in two shrill bursts. With a perfunctory brush down of the clay-stained overall she wore, she went to answer it.

A shock of recognition jolted her when she saw the tall, dark, well-dressed Spaniard on the doorstep. She was stunned into silence, her tongue clinging to the roof of her dry mouth. Bathed in spring sunshine, luxuriant ebony hair ruffled by the breeze, lean, bronzed classic features set in serious lines, he was devastatingly handsome.

'May I come in?' Leandro studied her intently. She had turned pale, her shock at his appearance palpable. Emerald eyes bright as jewels glanced evasively off his, her wealth of black curls tumbling down past slight shoulders now rigid with tension. She was wearing a shapeless garment liberally daubed with clay.

'Why? What do you want?'

Leandro quirked a brow at her intonation. She was a rough diamond in the manners department. 'To see you—what else?'

Molly let him in only because she didn't want to start an argument with him on the doorstep. He had no right to come to her home, a voice screamed inside her head. She felt cornered and her brain cells felt as though they had been frozen into inactivity. When she caught a glimpse of the vast car sitting out on the street, her jaw simply dropped. 'Does that limousine belong to you?'

'Sì…yes.' Leandro settled the ice bucket he was carrying into her hands, startling her. 'I thought we could share a drink.'

Dumbfounded by the gesture and clutching the bucket awkwardly, Molly stared fixedly down at the bottle protruding from the ice. It was very expensive bubbly, the very best: Bollinger Blanc de Noir. 'It's the middle of the day,' she muttered helplessly.

'So?' Brilliant dark eyes with a mesmeric glimmer of gold nailed hers head-on when she was least prepared for the collision. Her tummy flipped, butterflies fluttered and dangerous warmth surged between her thighs.

For a terrifying moment she was out of control of her body and the surge of memories that she had worked so hard to suppress engulfed her in a relentless tide. But now here he was in the flesh and suddenly she was remembering his weight on her, the raw burn of his sexual possession and the wild, hot excitement of it. 'Join me for lunch, *querida.*'

'No, I'm firing stuff…in the kiln,' Molly extended unevenly. Prompted by a defiant streak of vanity, she set down the ice bucket and began to remove her overall.

Leandro thrust the front door uneasily shut behind him. His lacklustre surroundings had already shot him out of his comfort zone. 'So this is where you live,' he remarked, a lean shapely hand encompassing the dreary hallway, which was no more than a narrow passage to provide access to the rooms. Like the ugly urban street outside and the tired furnishings, it spoke of a poverty he seldom saw and had certainly never experienced.

'How on earth did you find out where I lived?' Molly questioned tautly, pushing open the door of her bedroom and going in, only because she felt trapped standing so close to a male as tall and well built as Leandro in a confined area. The lounge was Jez's private space and always messily awash with dismantled car parts, motocross magazines and beer cans.

Leandro immediately saw her personality in the vibrant splashes of colour in the room. A multicoloured earthenware parrot plaque adorned the wall next to an oriental screen. The bed was draped with a vivid blue embroidered silk shawl. The floorboards had been painted white. An onion-shaped vase with a distinctive iridescent glaze drew his attention and he lifted it. 'Yours?' he asked.

Her smile, for she was pleased that he had guessed

that the piece was hers, lit her heart-shaped face with a glow of warmth that ensured she retained his attention.

Leandro relived the sensation of that lush ripe mouth pleasuring him and almost grabbed her into his arms there and then. Breathing in deep, hanging onto control of his rebellious body by a hair's breadth, he watched her step out of her flat shoes and into a pair of peep-toe polka-dot high heels that only accentuated the eccentricity of her attire. His devouring gaze zeroed in on the star tattoo etched above one fragile ankle. She wore a short black floral print dress belted to her tiny waist and black leggings that stretched only to mid-calf. Yet even though his tastes had never run to the Bohemian and he was a very conventional guy, he thought she looked incredibly sexy.

'You didn't tell me how you found out where I lived,' Molly reminded him.

'No, I didn't, did I?' Leandro fielded, his attention torn between the charms of her voluptuous mouth and the shadowy cleft visible between her high breasts when he gazed down at her. 'I had you followed home that morning—'

'You did…*what*?' Molly gasped in shock.

His level dark gaze had an unrepentant gleam. 'I told you that I wasn't prepared to lose you again, *gatita*.'

'But *followed*? By whom?'

'My security team.'

'Just how rich are you?' Molly whispered, her incredulity unhidden.

'I'll never go hungry,' Leandro quipped. 'And when I find you living like this, it only makes me more determined than ever to look after you.'

Molly lifted her chin, feline green eyes flashing an

acid shade of warning in his direction as she squared up to him. 'Only children need looking after—'

'Or very beautiful women,' Leandro, who had never suffered from a lack of assurance, ignored her aggressive stance and closed his hands to her shoulders to draw her closer.

'I didn't want to see you again. I made that quite clear,' Molly told him bluntly.

Leandro backed her up against the wall and pinned her there, his hands closing over hers to imprison her. Ensnared by scorching dark golden eyes, Molly could barely get breath into her straining lungs. Her awareness of the raw masculinity of his lean powerful body soared sky-high. Her nipples pinched tight beneath her clothes, erotic heat tingling low in her pelvis. '*Dios mio!*' he growled in urgent contradiction. 'You little liar. You did want to see me again and right now, you're burning up for me.'

Molly's knees were wobbling, but she continued to fight. 'You have quite an opinion of yourself—'

'Why not?' His brilliant eyes burned with unholy amusement as he bent down to her level to murmur huskily, his breath stirring the curls at her temples, 'Didn't you give me good cause that night?'

A hot, mortifying wave of guilty pink washed Molly's delicate features. 'I don't want to talk about that—'

'Talking in the bedroom is a heavily overrated pursuit, *querida*.' With a hungry groan of impatience, Leandro hauled her up to him and crushed her soft, pouting lips with ravenous urgency beneath his. As he banded both arms about her slight body to hold her to him she wrapped her arms round his neck, her breath rasping in her throat and her heart pounding inside her chest. She had forgotten how incredible he tasted and the sheer extent of the primal rush of excitement he could induce just by plunging his tongue into her mouth. He did it again and again too, racking her with desire and enforcing his sensual dominance.

There was no thought of denial in Molly's head. His deep drugging kisses and the lancing invasion of his tongue destroyed her defences and brought her treacherous body stingingly back to life. She wanted more. She told herself that in a couple of minutes she would push him away, tell him to leave, spell out the news that he had picked on the wrong woman. Just another minute, she bargained helplessly with herself while his skilful hands shaped the tender thrust of her breasts and sent a piercing arrow of longing zinging from her sensitised nipples to the damp core at the heart of her.

She writhed under him, frustrated by the barrier of their clothes. Her hunger for him was like a leaping flame tormenting her from inside her own skin. And evidently fully aware of the unbearable ache that was building up inside her, he cupped her mound beneath the leggings, making her gasp and moan and part her slender thighs in encouragement. The power of her own wanton response shattered her.

'You want me very much, *gatita*,' Leandro husked thickly, his hot appreciative gaze pinned to her. 'And you make me want as I didn't know I could want all the time.'

All the time, three crucial little words that jolted Molly, for she was facing the same challenge. She couldn't get him out of her head, day or night. It was as if she had caught a virus for which there was no cure. He pressed his mouth to the unbelievably tender skin below her ear and used the graze of his teeth to make her gasp and quiver, while he fought through layers of clinging fabric to touch her where she most craved his touch. Her spine arched, her body jackknifing, a cry of helpless pleasure escaping her when he found the hot, moist cleft that revealed her response. She was desperate for his caresses, her breath sobbing in her throat while she twisted and turned beneath the sensuous stroke of his fingers. The excitement built so fast she couldn't catch up with it. Instead she was wholly at the mercy of exquisite sensation while the knot of need tightening low in her stomach coiled ever tighter.

'Stop fighting it,' Leandro urged rawly, devouring the expressions on her passion-glazed features and the thrashing abandonment of her excitement.

She couldn't find a voice to answer him with. Control was long gone. He pushed a single finger into her tight entrance and suddenly she lost it completely, flying into the sun with an ecstatic cry while ripples of ever-spreading wondrous pleasure spread out from her pelvis to engulf her entire trembling body. A split second later she went into shock at what she had allowed to happen.

'Before I bury myself in your beautiful body, there's a conversation we really must have, *querida*,' Leandro purred. 'I'll get the champagne.'

With frantic hands, Molly put her clothing back in order while her treacherous body continued to sing and tingle with sensual euphoria. She was convinced she would never look Leandro in the face again. She had intended to throw him out and instead she had allowed him to give her a mind-blowing orgasm. There was no explaining that, no going back from that point to a claim of coolness. He had made a bonfire of her nonsensical rejection and trampled her pride in the ashes.

'Glasses?' Leandro prompted silkily when he reappeared to set the ice bucket down on the dresser.

Shame engulfing her in a tidal wave, Molly slid off the bed in an eel-like motion. 'I realise that I'm giving you very mixed messages, but I really don't want to go to bed with you again,' she proclaimed in a tight defensive tone.

Leandro dealt her an amused appraisal, knowing that he would cherish the past few minutes for a very long time. She was blushing like a schoolgirl, her lack of sophistication never more obvious to him or more appealing. 'I'm not fixated on beds, *querida*. The way I'm feeling right now, anywhere will do, any *way*,' he savoured softly, heightening her colour with his intimate tone. 'Glasses?'

'I don't have any.' Molly backed away from the bed much as if it was the scene of the crime. 'What was the conversation you said we had to have?'

Leandro tensed at that timely reminder and then breathed in deep. 'On the night that we met I didn't use condoms when we made love. Are you using any contraception?'

Molly stared at him, alarm bells jangling noisily inside her head in tune with startled shock waves of dismay and anger. 'No,' she admitted tightly. 'But I assumed that *you* did.'

'I'm afraid not, but I think it's unlikely that you will conceive,' Leandro admitted in a calm, dismissive tone of finality that only inflamed her temper more. 'I assume you have no idea one way or the other as yet?'

'You assume right and I'm glad to know that you're not losing any sleep over the risks you took with *my* body and *my* future!' Molly slung at him in furious attack. 'But the risk of falling pregnant is not just something that I can shrug off and hope for the best about. How could you be so careless?'

His lean, strong face was unreadable, his brilliant dark eyes semi-screened by his luxuriant black fringe of lashes. 'It took two of us to be careless,' he reminded her drily.

Molly threw her head back abruptly as though he had slapped her. 'You're a lot more experienced than I am. I was in an unfamiliar situation and I just didn't think of that angle—what's your excuse?'

Leandro shot her a sardonic appraisal. 'I don't make excuses. I made an oversight for which I apologise. If there's a problem, we'll face it together and I will give you my full support, but I seriously doubt that that necessity will arise.'

Molly wondered angrily why he was so infuriatingly confident that there would not be consequences. Did he lead a charmed life in which nothing ever went badly wrong for him? He had made love to her three times. Didn't he appreciate that she was young and fertile?

'I do not want to be pregnant!' she told him vehemently. 'In fact the very idea of it terrifies me—'

'This is my problem as well,' Leandro cut in forcefully.

'But I can't dismiss it as easily as you appear to. Maybe because I know that the world is not a forgiving place for a child who is born against other people's wishes, a child whose very existence may cause offence—'

His ebony brows had pleated in a bemused frown as she became increasingly emotional. '*Qué demonios*? What are you trying to say to me?'

'I'm illegitimate and the result of my mother's affair with someone else's husband,' Molly spelt out grittily, her slim hands tightening into taut fists of constraint by her sides. 'My mother died when I was nine and my grandmother took charge of my older half-sister and me. My sister was born within a marriage. My grandmother handed me over to social services for adoption because, as far as she was concerned, I was an embarrassment who should never have been born.'

Leandro was more unsettled than he was prepared to admit by that sad little tale. He knew that births had been concealed and most probably worse had happened in his own family's history over the centuries. He also knew that even in today's more liberal society, respectability and other people's opinions still remained his mother's most pressing concern. She kept his younger sister, Julieta, on a tight social leash, fearful that too much freedom would lead to embarrassing media headlines.

'I'm sorry that you had that experience—'

'Talk's cheap!' Molly sizzled back at him. 'But I don't want any child of mine to suffer that kind of rejection.'

'There won't be a child. Let's tackle trouble if it comes, not look for it in advance,' Leandro advised drily.

'But what are you going to do if I *am* pregnant?' Molly spun away, her voice shrill with her angry distress, for she knew that the fragile foundations of her security would be utterly destroyed by the advent of single parenthood. She worked unsocial hours in a casual job without prospects. There was no room for childcare in her tight budget, no supportive family circle to help out and she knew all too well how hard it was to raise children alone, for hadn't her birth mother failed dismally at the same task?

'We'll tackle that when and if it happens. Are you always such a pessimist?' Leandro enquired with silken derision, exasperated by her angry attack over the risk of something that he was convinced was unlikely to happen. 'Such a tragedy-queen?'

A furious flush lit Molly's cheeks at that crack and she stepped forward. 'How dare you?' she snapped. 'This is my life we're talking about in the balance, not yours. So I want to know where I stand. Why shouldn't I? I'm pretty sure that the best you'll offer me in a tight corner will be the cash for a termination!'

His lean, darkly handsome face clenched with distaste. A storm of outrage roared through Leandro. 'How dare you make such an assumption?' he demanded in a seething undertone. 'That is not how I would behave.'

'Well, whatever!' Molly shot back at him, her furious distress undiminished by that assurance. 'Let's hope we never have to explore that predicament.'

Leandro had had more than enough drama for one morning and he refused to be the ongoing target of her resentment and disdain. His lean, strong face was etched into forbidding lines and his stunning eyes were hot with indignation. 'When are you planning to take responsibility for your own behaviour? And stop trying to blame me for it?'

Mortified colour washed Molly's face, for he hit right home with that rejoinder. 'Right now, all I want is for you to leave—'

'Don't worry,' Leandro derided. 'I have no desire to stay.'

Just at that moment the bedroom door opened and framed Jez's broad, solid frame. He stared at her and Leandro with frowning blue eyes. 'Why are you shouting, Molly? What's going on in here?'

'Leandro was just about to leave,' Molly snapped.

'I'm Jez Andrews, Molly's friend,' Jez addressed Leandro while at the same time taking up a protective stance beside Molly. 'I think you should do as she asks and go now.'

Leandro was taken aback by the sudden appearance of another male and aggressive instincts threatened his rigid self-discipline. He was quick to recognise the possessive light in the younger man's expression. Annoyance and suspicion slivered through Leandro, for it was not only obvious that Molly and Jez lived below the same roof but also that they were on familiar terms with each other.

'You know how to get in touch with me if you need to,' Leandro drawled in a tone of pure ice.

Molly was frozen where she stood until she heard the slam of the front door. Then she crumpled and tears rained down her face. Even while she fought to get a grip on herself, all the pent-up emotions of recent days were taking their toll and overflowing. Unused to her crying, Jez wrapped his arms round her in an awkward hug.

'Who on earth was that bloke?' Jez demanded when she had calmed down a little. 'And what's he got to do with you?'

After that, the whole story came tumbling out because Molly was so unnerved by the fear that she might fall pregnant she just had to get her feelings off her chest there and then. Before her reddened eyes,

Jez's expression grew more and more censorious. Although he said nothing and uttered no criticism, his surprise at her behaviour spoke volumes and pierced her pride. He was, however, a good deal more vocal when it came to Leandro.

'A girl like you doesn't belong in a limo.' Jez saw her wince and hastened to add, 'A bloke with that kind of money could only be messing around with you because he's bored with his own kind.'

Jez had a shrewd streak about people that Molly respected. 'Imagine asking me to be his mistress, though!' she framed with a humourless laugh. 'Do I look the ornamental type?'

'I wish I'd thumped him,' Jez growled, unamused. 'You can do a hell of a lot better than him—'

'Not if I fall pregnant,' Molly interposed with a shiver of fear. 'If I end up with a baby my whole life and my prospects go right down the tubes. I'll never stop struggling to survive.'

'Let's hope for the best,' Jez advised stonily, his face tightening while he considered that possibility. 'You know, I always used to think that eventually you and I might get together.'

Molly settled dismayed eyes on him, for it had never occurred to her that he might look on her as anything other than an honorary sister. 'But we're *friends*—'

'Yes, well.' Jez shrugged defensively. 'Why shouldn't friendship be the first step in something more? We get on well. We know each other right through. There'd be no nasty surprises. It would have made a lot of sense.'

'Don't say any more,' Molly urged unhappily, for she had never once considered Jez in that light. 'All you're doing is reminding me that getting involved with Leandro was like giving way to a sudden attack of madness.'

'No point beating yourself up about it,' the heavily built blond man pointed out in a tone of practicality. 'That won't change anything.'

Molly attended two craft fairs that weekend and the sale of several pieces of pottery lifted her spirits. As the following week wore on her mood steadily declined when her menstrual cycle failed to deliver the reassurance she sought. She was working long hours and her usual energy seemed strangely absent. She began feeling incredibly tired at about the same time as she started feeling nauseous and off her food. Anxiety took her over then, because she feared the worst and the shadows below her eyes deepened while she lay awake at night fretting. She was planning to go out and buy a pregnancy test when Jez persuaded her to go to the doctor instead to get a more reliable diagnosis.

The doctor was very thorough and he assured her that there was no doubt that she was carrying her first child. Although Molly had believed she was prepared for that possibility, she was devastated when her biggest fear was confirmed. Jez phoned her from his workshop to ask the result and she gave it in a deadened voice, staring at her reflection in the hall mirror while she tried and failed to imagine her slender body swollen with pregnancy.

A baby, a real living, breathing, crying baby, would be looking to her for total support in less than nine months' time. A termination wasn't an option for her. Her own mother had given her the chance of life in equally unpromising circumstances and Cathy had done her best, even if her best hadn't been that great. Could she herself do any less for her own child? She dug out Leandro's business card and decided to send him a text message, because she really couldn't face speaking to him just at that moment and when they had parted on such bad terms.

'I need to see you URGENTLY.'

In the conference room of the Carrera bank where he was involved in a meeting, Leandro read the message and appreciated the appeal of the block capitals. He was convinced that she had discovered that she was not pregnant and now wanted to tell him that she was sorry for making such a fuss. He walked into his office to phone her.

'Join me for dinner tonight,' he suggested. 'I'll send a car to pick you up at eight.'

Molly winced at the prospect of breaking her news over a dining table and then scolded herself for caring about such a triviality. He was as much to blame as she was for the development, so why was she getting all worked up at the prospect of telling him?

When Jez came home from work, he joined her in the kitchen. 'How do you feel?' he enquired awkwardly.

'Like I want to kick myself for being so stupid,' she told him truthfully.

'Have you told *him* yet?'

'I'm telling Leandro tonight—not that I expect that will make much difference to my plans—'

'You already have plans?' Jez queried.

'Just getting on with life as best I can,' Molly muttered dully.

Jez reached for her hand where it was clenched on the edge of the sink. 'But you don't have to do it alone…'

Molly looked up him uncertainly. 'What do you mean?'

Jez breathed in slow and deep. 'I've thought hard about this since we had our conversation, so take a minute and think about it before you say no. I'm willing to marry you and bring up the kid as my own—'

Molly was astonished by that suggestion. 'Jez, for goodness sake, I wouldn't let you sacrifice yourself like that—'

'I want to help, Molly. Together we could make a good team,' the blond man reasoned earnestly. 'I'm not expecting you to love me but, in time, I'm sure we'd become closer.'

Tears were clogging Molly's throat and she was too choked up to speak. His generosity was almost too much for her to bear. She grasped both his hands in hers and squeezed them to express her feelings. But for the first time she didn't feel she could say anything she liked to Jez because she now knew that he thought of her as more than a friend and cherished hopes that she could not fulfil. She loved and trusted him, but she wasn't attracted to him and felt that anything other than platonic friendship would be doomed by that fact.

'You're too kind for your own good,' she told him chokily and she went off to get dressed, feeling more than ever as though her security was breaking up beneath her feet. How could she possibly remain living in Jez's home now? It wouldn't be fair to him if she stayed on. He was too involved in her life and it wasn't healthy. He was less likely to make the effort to meet someone else while she was still around, she acknowledged unhappily.

Dead on the hour of eight, a uniformed chauffeur rang the bell to tell her that the limousine was waiting for her…

CHAPTER FIVE

LEANDRO watched Molly cross the restaurant. Male heads turned and followed her progress. Her dress was unremarkable, fitted enough to hug her rounded breasts and just short enough to reveal shapely knees and accentuate the high heels she favoured to combat her diminutive height. But the men didn't stop looking and neither did he. Maybe it was that eye-catching waterfall of jet-black curls, the enormous emerald green eyes and that full quivering pink mouth that he only had to look at to get hard and ready. A woman hadn't affected him that way since the teenage years when fantasy had driven his hormones and that simple fact still annoyed the hell out of him.

'This is a really fashionable place,' Molly remarked unevenly, striving not to stare at him and allow his magnetic attraction to influence her. But he looked drop dead gorgeous in a light grey suit and sky blue silk tie and her heartbeat quickened to a trot and her pulses quickened even before she sat down at the quiet corner table.

'I often eat here in the evening. It's quicker than ordering food in,' Leandro responded. 'You look beautiful, *querida*.'

Stiff as an iron bar trying to bend, Molly rearranged the salt and pepper and shook her head in immediate disagreement. 'No, I don't. I assumed you'd want to eat somewhere quieter, the sort of place we could talk.'

Talk? Leandro did not like the ominous sound of that word. His needs and wishes were the height of masculine simplicity: he wanted to feast his eyes on her and take her home with him at the end of the meal. Her cloaked appraisal, however, set his even white teeth on edge and made him commence their meal with a leading question. 'Isn't it time you told me about Jez?'

Alerted by the tough edge to his tone, Molly lifted her head from the menu she was studying. 'Why do you think that?'

His dark eyes were hard as granite. 'You're obviously on very familiar terms with him. How does he fit into your life?'

'He's my best friend,' Molly confided. 'He owns the house so he's also my landlord.'

Leandro had never had much faith in platonic male and female friendships and his conviction that Jez had a more personal interest in Molly was not dispelled by that explanation. 'He behaved more like a man guarding his turf and warning off the competition—like a boyfriend.'

Uneasy colour warmed her cheeks. It bothered her that Leandro had only had to meet Jez once to immediately question the calibre of their friendship. Was that a tribute to Leandro's shrewd grasp of human nature? Or a sign that he was the jealous type? 'Jez is very fond of me,' she said defensively, 'but there's never been anything else between us. We've known each other since we were in foster care together as kids.'

'I thought you were adopted,' Leandro countered.

'Not for very long. I was older—there weren't many takers. An older couple who already had a son took me because they wanted a daughter. My adoptive father died of a heart attack six months after I moved in,' Molly explained ruefully. 'My adoptive mother got very depressed and decided she had enough to handle without taking on an extra child. I was back in foster care by the end of the year.'

Leandro could only think of his own privileged childhood. He had been encouraged to believe that, as heir to a massive estate and centuries of proud heritage, he was the most important little person in the household. Long, lonely stretches at boarding school had contrasted with an excess of luxury and attention during the holidays.

'That must have been hard on you,' he remarked.

Molly lifted and dropped a thin shoulder. 'I survived. I'm quite a strong character, Leandro. I don't think you see that in me.'

Leandro measured the resolute angle of her pointed chin and the light of challenge in her clear gaze and vented a sardonic laugh of disagreement. He wondered how he had contrived to stumble on one of the very few young women in Europe who wouldn't snatch at the opportunity to have a billionaire make all her material dreams come true. 'Don't I?' he traded drily. 'I find you very argumentative.'

At that inopportune moment the waiter appeared to pour the wine. Annoyed by Leandro's censure, Molly put a hand over her glass and requested a soda and lime instead. When they were alone again, she snapped, 'I am *not* argumentative!'

'I don't stage rows in public places,' Leandro deliv-

ered with contemptuous cool. 'Raise your voice again
and I walk out of here.'

'I really could throw something at you at this
moment,' Molly confided in a shaken undertone; she was
taken aback by the sizzling strength of her annoyance.

'Don't try that either,' Leandro warned her with a
freezing glance that chilled her fury with the efficiency
of a bucket of ice.

'In my experience, most men walk the other way
when things get difficult,' Molly rejoined with a
scornful shift of her dark head.

'I'm incredibly tough.' His strong jaw line hardened
while his brilliant dark golden eyes lit on her like
burning flames. 'Your problem is that you want me but
you can't handle it, *gatita*.'

'That is absolutely not true!' Molly protested, staring
back at him in as frozen a manner as she could contrive
while desperate to get the dialogue back on track.

'The truth can hurt,' Leandro drawled smooth as silk,
thick black lashes low over his acute gaze.

Molly shifted like a butterfly stabbed by a display
pin. 'Haven't you already guessed why I contacted
you?' she pressed, the tip of her tongue stealing out to
moisten her plump lower lip.

That little play with her tongue sent an erotic thrill
arrowing straight to Leandro's groin. 'You were keen
to reassure me that you're fine and we have nothing to
worry about?' he suggested.

Molly tensed at that unfortunate misinterpretation.
'No, I'm not fine in the way that you mean.'

The waiter reappeared to take their order while
Leandro wondered what on earth she was talking about
because he could not believe that she might be pregnant.

'Meaning?' he prompted.

Molly could not comprehend why he was being so obtuse. 'Isn't it obvious? I saw a doctor today, Leandro. I'm going to have a baby!'

Leandro studied her in brooding silence, transfixed by that staggering claim. He had almost but not quite come to terms with the suspicion that he was infertile and would never father a child. He had planned to go for tests some time and find out for sure. Molly's announcement hit him like a bolt from the blue and stunned him. His lean, darkly handsome face clenched and he paled as he studied her, marvelling at her words while wondering what she could possibly hope to gain from a lie.

'All right, so you're shocked. Well, so was I, but there's no doubt and no mistake. I am very definitely pregnant,' Molly spelt out, enunciating each word of that affirmation with care.

Leandro veiled his stunned eyes. Was it possible that he could father a child? It was true that Aloise had failed to conceive, but his late wife had also refused to pursue the matter with her gynaecologist. Could one random night turn his world upside down? Could Molly's tiny frame be carrying his baby? For a split second, a primitive leap of satisfaction and relief lanced through him that he was not, after all, unable to ensure the continuation of the family name. Squashing that leap of satisfaction, he surveyed her with impenetrable dark eyes, fierce tension thrumming through his big, powerful body. If she did prove to be pregnant, he would have to marry her for the baby's sake. He could see no other solution to the situation. Unfortunately, Leandro was in no hurry to marry again. One taste of freedom, he reflected grimly, and then it was gone. It was a shame that he hadn't made the most of his liberty while he still had it.

'Say something,' Molly urged unhappily.

'This is not the place to discuss such a private matter. We'll talk at my apartment after we've eaten.'

For the first time Molly fully appreciated how skilled Leandro was at controlling his emotions and concealing his reactions. No expression that she could interpret crossed his lean, bronzed features. That comprehensive reserve and self-discipline unnerved Molly, who wore her feelings on the surface and rarely hesitated to express them.

The fish course that Leandro had selected arrived at the table. Molly caught the aroma from the dish and it curdled her stomach and made her stiffen in dismay. 'Certain smells make me feel sick,' she confided.

And that was the last conversation they had for some time, for Molly fought the nausea until she could bear it no longer and then abandoned the table to flee to the cloakroom. Leandro took the hint and had the fish removed. The minutes ticked past. Eventually he asked one of the serving staff to check that Molly was all right. Soon afterwards she reappeared, looking pale as a wraith with shadows lying like faint purple bruises below her eyes.

'Sorry, I'm really not hungry now,' she muttered, pushing her plate away untouched.

Leandro suggested that they leave. She protested that he hadn't eaten. He said he wasn't hungry either and it was true. His appetite had vanished. He felt like the condemned man at his last supper and even that final meal had been denied him. But he knew what his duty was, and with a supportive arm banded to her slight figure, he escorted her out of the restaurant. Outside, he stilled in surprise when several cameras went off and Molly shrank in dismay against him. His security team had been caught unawares and had neglected to warn him because it was a long time since Leandro had done anything to attract the attention of the paparazzi. He was annoyed by that renewed interest at the optimum wrong moment in his life. It was certainly not the instant he would have chosen to introduce Molly to the public eye.

'I want you to see a doctor,' Leandro announced in the limo.

'It's just morning sickness—'

'It's half past nine in the evening,' he objected.

'Well, apparently it works like that with some people. It doesn't mean anything's wrong. I just have to put up with it,' she replied.

Leandro studied her slender figure. There wasn't much of her to study and concern assailed him, for she didn't seem strong enough to survive missing many meals. His innate sense of practicality was already processing the concept of making a second marriage and doing so at speed. What choice did he have? He owed a duty of care towards Molly and their unborn child. He owed it to his family name. But that didn't mean that he had to *like* the prospect of surrendering his freedom again. Even so, if he came out of it with the next generation in the family secured, perhaps it would be worth the sacrifice, he reasoned grimly.

Nervous as a cat, Molly watched Leandro restively pace the floor in the elegant main reception room of his apartment. The lights of the city illuminated the darkness beyond the floor-deep windows. He might not have said one word out of place, but even he could not hide his tension. She found it hard to look away from him. It seemed juvenile to her to still be thinking of how gorgeous he was, but she couldn't help it. His chiselled masculine features and his spectacular heavily lashed dark eyes grabbed her attention with embarrassing ease. Encountering her anxious gaze, he strode forward.

'Once you've had the pregnancy confirmed, we'll get married as soon as it can be arranged.'

Molly blinked in astonishment. 'You can't be serious. You hardly know me—'

'You're carrying my baby and it's expected. That's all I need to know for the moment. If the baby is a boy, he will be my heir and the next Duke of Sandoval—'

Her bright eyes widened in amazement. 'There's a title in your family?'

Leandro nodded.

'So who's the current duke?'

'I am, but I only use the title at home.'

Molly had suddenly become as stiff as if she had had a poker strapped to her spine. 'You're a duke...and you're asking me to marry you?'

'I'm not giving you a choice on this. You cannot bring up any child of mine alone,' Leandro breathed tautly. 'I want my child to grow up in my home with his family and to speak my language. We can only achieve that end by becoming man and wife.'

'But you're still getting over your last wife,' Molly mumbled. But as soon as she had spoken and noticed his face shadow she wished she had kept that thought to herself.

'I'm not an emotional man, *querida*. Nor do I make tasteless comparisons. I find you extremely attractive and see no reason why we shouldn't have a success-ful marriage.'

Unnerved by his dispassionate outlook, Molly shook her head slowly. 'I want to be loved by the man I marry.'

Leandro released his breath in a slow hiss of frustra-tion. 'I can't give you love,' he responded without hesita-tion.

He was a duke, a *real* Spanish duke, and Molly was horrified by that revelation, for she could not imagine how someone as ordinary as she believed herself to be could possibly become the wife of a man of such wealth and high status. 'I respect your sense of commitment towards the baby,' she told him tensely.

'And to you, *querida*,' Leandro added, reaching down to close her hands into his and urge her up out of her seat.

Her mouth ran dry as he drew her close. 'Only a couple of weeks ago the only thing you thought I was good enough for was being your mistress. If I couldn't even make it into the girlfriend category, how can you sincerely say that you want to marry me?'

Leandro was already picturing her in his gilded four-poster bed at the *castillo*, a seductive image that acted as an opportune sweetener to his reluctance to remarry. He stared down at her with hot dark golden eyes that made her feel overheated and dizzy. 'My libido isn't fussy about labels. I want you, regardless of who you are.'

Molly trembled in contact with his muscular, pow-erfully aroused body. He desired her and she could feel the unashamed evidence of his desire. But was a hunger that left her boneless sufficient to base a marriage on?

'It would be diplomatic to forget that I once invited you to be my mistress. If you're having my baby, that is no longer feasible,' Leandro completed.

'You're determined that the baby should have your name?'

'Do you want your child to be illegitimate?'

Molly lost colour and dropped her expressive eyes. 'No, I don't, but I don't want to make a hasty marriage that I live to regret either.'

Leandro surveyed her with considerable coolness, for he had expected—not unnaturally in his own opinion—a much more enthusiastic response to his proposal. Few women in her position would have hesitated. What was her problem? What was holding her back? The blond guy with the oil stains on his hands?

'There will be no possibility of a divorce,' Leandro added.

Molly was impressed rather than put off by that statement, for she didn't want to trust her future to a man likely to give up on his marital vows at the first hurdle. She didn't want empty promises from him either. But though he couldn't offer her love he could give her other things. Marriage to Leandro would bring financial security and every material advantage her child could ever want. Even more crucially, it would also give her child a father, indeed a normal two parent family. Possibly, she reflected uncertainly, she should be thinking about what such a marriage would do for their child, rather than what it would do for her on a more personal basis.

'Molly…what's your answer?' Leandro pressed.

Molly was all flustered. 'I need time to think—'

'But we haven't got time. What do you have to think about?' Leandro demanded imperiously.

'That you even ask that question reveals the depth of your arrogance,' Molly murmured tautly.

Dark eyes cold as ice, his fabulous bone structure hardened. 'I won't accept a negative response, *querida*. If you won't marry me, I'll be forced to fight you in court for custody of our child.'

The speed with which he resorted to that threat shocked Molly. Aware that he was watching her every move like a hawk, she backed away from him. 'Are you trying to intimidate me?'

'No. I'm telling you the truth. I'm telling you what will happen if you don't marry me. Do you expect me to lie?' Leandro raked back at her drily. 'You need all the facts before you can make a sensible decision.'

'You would actually try to take my baby away from me?' Molly was appalled by that threat that sunk like a deep chill into her bones.

Leandro closed a confident hand round her wrist to prevent her from retreating further. 'I think you're too sensible to go to the wall on this. I believe you'll reach the right decision for all of us.'

But his ruthlessness shook her rigid. She was as unprepared for it as she had been for the mistress proposition he had put to her two weeks earlier. Suddenly she was appreciating how misleading his cool façade and exquisite manners were. Below the skin, Leandro was every bit as aggressive, dominant and cruel in his instincts as a street fighter protecting his territory.

'I'd like to go home now,' she told him flatly.

'In the morning we'll have your pregnancy confirmed and you'll give me an answer. But first,' Leandro breathed, pulling her to him.

Molly meant to resist and imitate a wax dummy in his arms but the hot hard hunger of his sensual mouth and the erotic plunge of his tongue sent wanton excitement roaring through her in a relentless tidal wave. She clutched at his jacket to steady herself. She was out of breath and her knees were wobbling and a forbidden ache of emptiness was stirring between her slender thighs.

'You don't want to go home, *querida*,' Leandro murmured silkily.

Molly wanted to either slap him or scream at him, but knew that either response would merely make her look childish and out of control. He watched her with smouldering dark eyes and, although every treacherous fibre of her being urged her to fling herself back into his arms, she withstood the temptation. Unfortunately the thought of another night in bed with him banished all coherent thought and conscience and made her hate herself. Winning that mental battle with herself still felt like losing because he was right on one score: she didn't want to leave him.

Jez intercepted her in the hall when she walked through the front door. *'Well?'*

'Leandro asked me to marry him.'

Jez was visibly taken aback.

Molly registered that she was secretly pleased that Leandro had contrived to confound her friend's expectations. 'I said I'd give him my answer tomorrow.'

Jez grimaced. 'You're infatuated with him. You're hardly going to say no.'

Molly flung her head high. 'He's the father of my baby. Shouldn't I at least give him a chance?'

She couldn't get to sleep that night. Was she infatuated with Leandro Carrera Marquez? She supposed she was, because from the hour of their meeting she hadn't been able to get him out of her head for longer than five minutes. Lying there, she relived the fiery heat of his mouth on hers and discovered that it only made her long for a more intimate connection. Ashamed of her craving for his touch, she buried her face in the pillow. He had threatened her with a custody battle. He had made it very clear that he wanted the child she carried, whether it was born in or out of marriage, and shouldn't she respect him for that? She did not want to raise her child alone. She could not offer her baby the security, comfort or advantages that marriage to Leandro would bring. How could she possibly say no to him?

And yet to marry a man she hardly knew and move to another country, another culture, when she did not even speak the language would also be a great challenge. It certainly wouldn't be the easy option, she recognized heavily. In addition, she would be a second wife and she wasn't entirely sure that she fancied that role, of filling a position previously held by a predecessor. He had said comparisons were tasteless, but did that simply mean that she could not compare on any level to his first bride? Or was she being paranoid? Paranoid, Molly decided for herself. In truth she didn't want Leandro to have *ever* been with another woman, much less have cared enough to marry one.

He picked her up shortly after ten the following morning and accompanied her to an appointment with a gynaecologist in Harley Street. A pregnancy test confirmed what she already knew. She was scolded for being so thin, which annoyed her intensely since that was her natural state of being and she ate like a horse as a rule.

'You're not supposed to argue with your consultant,' Leandro censured when she climbed back into his limousine.

Molly tossed her head, black curls rippling across her shoulders 'Well, you did say how argumentative I was,' she reminded him flippantly. 'I'm small and skinny. I was *born* small and skinny, get used to it!'

'Will I be getting the opportunity…to get used to you being small and skinny?' Leandro enquired lazily, brilliant dark eyes nailed to her cross face. In a short-sleeved colourful blouse and a denim skirt, she looked barely old enough to be out of her teens and struck him as being almost as volatile.

Molly turned her head, emerald green eyes very bright and challenging. 'You didn't give me much choice when you threatened to go to court for a custody battle—'

'So, that's a *yes*?'

Still playing it cool and unconcerned, Molly shrugged agreement.

'I'm not very fond of weddings,' Leandro admitted with a crashing lack of tact. 'I'd like a discreet church ceremony to be held here with only witnesses present before we fly straight out to Spain.'

Molly was not impressed. He didn't seem to care about what she might want. So he had been married before and all that bridal hoopla was a bore to him, but she was hoping to only marry once and she would have preferred a proper wedding. Impervious to her lack of enthusiasm, he took her to an exclusive jeweler to choose wedding rings. Lunch at an exclusive hotel followed. But by then her silence was really getting on his nerves. 'What's wrong with you?' he asked icily.

'You're so bossy, it's intolerable. I don't know whether I'm back at school or in prison because you never stop telling me what to do and how things will be,' she complained.

'You should speak up,' declared the man who had already called her argumentative. 'I have a naturally authoritative streak.'

'I'm naturally defiant.'

Leandro dealt her a measuring look. 'Then we will clash.'

But over the following ten days there was little chance of the prospective bride and groom clashing because Leandro returned to Spain on business and occasional phone calls were their only means of communication. Generally, an aide passed on Leandro's instructions during his absence. She signed a prenuptial agreement, gave up her job and began packing up her life in London. Leandro sent her a credit card and told her go shopping for an outfit for the wedding and also clothes to wear in a warmer climate. She went to Harrods and bought herself a wedding dress with his money. He had suggested something, 'elegant and sober', but she ignored his advice completely and fell for a white lace corset top teamed with a gloriously full skirt and towering high-heeled shoes.

When she got home that day she found an intriguing letter in her post. From a leading City lawyers' office, it invited her to attend an appointment to discuss a confidential matter. Curious about why such mystery should be necessary, she rang to make enquiries but could gain no further information on the phone.

'Do you think it might be someone in your birth family trying to get in touch with you?' Jez enquired. 'Or an inheritance from them?'

'I doubt it. There was only my sister and my grandmother left, and she handed me over to social services,' she reminded him ruefully.

But curiosity and her undeniable hope that against all odds her relatives *were* attempting to reconnect with her ensured that Molly attended the appointment. She was shown into a smart office and greeted by Elena Carson, a svelte lawyer in her thirties, who invited her to take a seat.

'I understand you're soon to be married, Miss Chapman.'

'Yes.' Molly frowned, immediately wondering how the other woman had come by that information and why it was even being mentioned.

'I must ask you to be patient while I explain why you've been invited to come here today,' the brunette advanced smoothly. 'My client wishes to remain anonymous and has engaged me to approach you with a generous financial offer.'

'A *financial* offer?' Molly questioned in bewilderment. Disappointment settled over her like a fog that blocked the sunlight. Self-evidently, the appointment had nothing to do with her blood relatives and she felt foolish for ever having cherished the hope that it had.

'My client wants to stop your marriage taking place,' Elena Carson explained.

Struggling to focus on that startling admission, Molly gave the brunette a stunned appraisal. '*Stop* my marriage?'

'My client is aware that it would be a very advantageous marriage from your point of view and is willing to give you a large sum of money to compensate you for changing your mind,' the lawyer delivered calmly.

In shock, Molly parted dry lips and slowly folded them shut again. Someone wanted to pay her not to marry Leandro? Who? A member of his family? Another woman with designs on him?

'I'm not interested in changing my mind,' she replied without hesitation. 'Have you thought about how hard it might be to fit into a titled Spanish family, who can trace their ancestors back to the fifteenth century? Have you thought about how difficult it might be to live up to your future husband's high standards?'

Molly was steadily reddening with anger. 'I don't want to listen to any more of this nonsense. If Leandro was a king, I would feel equal to the challenge, because he is the father of my baby and I assume that he knew exactly what he was doing when he asked me to be his wife!' she heard herself proclaim heatedly, only to inwardly squirm a second later at what she had given away with that outburst.

The other woman, however, did not bat an eyelash. 'My client wants to act in everyone's best interests and recognises that you would be making a considerable sacrifice in choosing not to go ahead with the marriage—'

'Oh, does he…or is it, does she?' Molly interrupted furiously as she shot to her feet.

'And on that basis is prepared to offer you two million pounds towards making a new life for yourself somewhere else and never contacting Mr Carrera Marquez again,' the older woman stated with complete cool.

'As I'm not marrying Leandro for his money, you can't use money as a bribe to persuade me not to marry him!' Molly proclaimed with angry pride.

'That was not my client's intent, Miss Chapman. My client is aware that you are expecting a child and wishes to ensure that both you and your child will enjoy a secure future. You should consider the offer. It has been suggested that if you sign or have already signed a pre-nuptial agreement with your fiancé, you might well receive a great deal less money in any divorce settlement.'

Having signed such an agreement a couple of days previously, Molly was well aware of that fact. In short, any act of adultery, desertion or what was hazily termed 'unreasonable behaviour' during the course of their marriage would result in her instant impoverishment. But Molly was desperate to know who was prepared to offer such a vast amount of money to prevent her from marrying Leandro in the first place. The solicitor, however, refused to divulge that information. It outraged Molly to be kept in the dark when it was obvious that what she considered to be her own private business was clearly very far from being private. How many people had Leandro told about her pregnancy? And if she informed him about the offer that had been made to her, would he know who was behind it?

With only forty-eight hours to go before the wedding, Molly barely slept that night while she agonised over whether or not to tell Leandro. What if it was someone in his own family who was trying to buy her off and persuade her to disappear? With the kind of money involved she could only think that the culprit was most likely to be a close relative of his. Leandro would be outraged. Did she really want to risk causing that amount of trouble and strife within the family circle before she even arrived in Spain? Would it not be wiser to keep quiet for the moment and give people the chance to at least get to know her first…?

CHAPTER SIX

MOLLY examined her reflection in the wardrobe mirror from every angle.

Certainly Leandro would not be able to accuse her of looking insufficiently bridal. She had purchased every frivolous piece of finery possible for the occasion, right down to the filmy underwear and the lace garter adorned with a blue ribbon. Her dress was a fairy-tale dream of fluid organza styled over matt satin. The glass beading and metallic embroidery on the basque bodice and full skirt caught and reflected the light. Diamanté butterfly combs confined her mane of curls to the back of her head and, keen not to overdo the frills, she had added nothing else.

'Are you ready?' Jez asked. 'The limo driver is panicking. But, you know, it's not too late to change your mind.'

'I know what I'm doing,' Molly told her oldest friend. 'I want my baby to have what I never had—a *proper* home and a family.'

'Let's hope Leandro is up to the challenge,' the blond man responded drily.

'I don't think he'd be so keen to marry me if he

wasn't,' Molly answered, striving to look more positive than she actually felt. The offer of a bribe not to marry Leandro had seriously dented her confidence. Was it possible that she was unsuitable as a wife for him?

Jez had agreed to act as a witness at the ceremony. Molly was glad to have her friend's support as the limo ferried them through the traffic to the church. The photographer Molly had engaged for the occasion snapped her on the church steps with her bouquet of pink rose buds and her lucky horseshoe favour and told her that she had a lovely smile. Her heartbeat was pounding frantically fast at the base of throat when she walked down the aisle with a hand braced on Jez's arm. Leandro, accompanied only by one other man, awaited her at the altar. Sheathed in a charcoal-grey pinstripe suit, which he'd teamed with an immaculate white shirt, he looked breathtakingly handsome.

Leandro, still recovering from the unexpected ordeal of having to pose or the photographer who had intercepted him outside, surveyed Molly, who looked every inch the blushing bride. Her green eyes were luminous pools in her delicate face, her pink mouth as lush as the roses she carried and as full of sensual appeal as the creamy swell of her rounded breasts above the neckline of her romantic dress. As she knelt down by his side it was a challenge for him to take his eyes from her and the tightness at his groin merely intensified.

Molly spoke her vows in a clear voice that betrayed nothing of the nervous butterflies in her tummy. She was fiercely aware of Leandro's proximity. She allowed her gaze to linger on his hard, bronzed profile and felt her pulses leap when he turned lustrous dark eyes on her as they exchanged rings. He was her husband now, she thought with a rush of disbelief at the concept when the ceremony ended. He introduced her to his lawyer, who had acted as his witness, and it took her aback that he had not asked a friend to perform the office as she had.

Both witnesses declined the invitation to join them for lunch. Jez gave her an emotional hug as he knew they were flying straight out to Spain after their meal.

'I can't believe we're married,' Molly told Leandro chattily over the lunch, which was served in a hotel suite. Having been too nauseous to eat earlier in the day, she now made up for it with a healthy appetite.

In comparison, Leandro had felt married from the instant he'd walked into the church. He was already fighting off an oppressive sense of confinement, which had not been helped by his mother's hysterical last-minute phone call pleading with him to change his mind while assuring him that he would live to regret making the biggest mistake of his life. Perhaps he had been too optimistic in expecting his family to see the sound good sense of his decision. After all, a pregnant bride met two of their expectations at once. He remained uneasily conscious, however, that when he looked at Molly her radiance and glorious curves grabbed him first and made her fertility status the very last thing on his mind.

'I suppose I'd better get changed,' she said, rising from the table.

'No…keep the dress on, *querida*.'

Molly's brows pleated. 'For the flight?'

'Why not?' Dark golden eyes hot with hunger, Leandro closed a hand over hers to pull her close and savour the fresh lemony scent that he had come to associate with her presence. 'I want to take it off you. You can change before we land.'

Colour turned her cheeks poppy-red. His sensual appraisal sent raw sexual awareness shooting through her in a responsive wave. Her nipples swelled and damp heat stirred between her thighs. He had taught her to want him and, although it annoyed her a great deal, she couldn't yet keep a lid on her desire for his touch.

'What was your last wedding like?' Molly asked on the way to the airport, while gritting her teeth and refusing to look at him. The question had been hovering at the back of her mind all day and she had kicked it off her tongue a dozen times before finally sacrificing her pride and voicing it.

Leandro froze as if she had turned a gun on him. 'I don't think we should discuss that.'

Offended by his reticence, Molly sent him a glimmering look of suspicion. 'Why not?'

Leandro breathed in deep. 'It was different—a big society wedding.'

And that was it, one sentence and he fell silent. Nevertheless, he had said enough to satisfy her curiosity. Molly wished she hadn't asked, for she was making all the tasteless comparisons he would have condemned. He had pushed out the boat without complaint for his first marriage, which really told her all she needed to know about how he viewed his second excursion into matrimony. But, then, hadn't he already displayed his indifference to her feelings most effectively? He hadn't once smiled or paid her a single compliment on the day when all women expected to feel special.

A lot of people turned to stare at her in her wedding dress at the airport. Molly ignored them, but she could

feel how much Leandro disliked the scrutiny. His lean,
dark features settled into grim lines and his silences got
more extended. It didn't help when his security team
weren't quick enough to prevent a photographer from
stepping into their path and taking a flash photo of
them.

'You should have let me get changed,' Molly told
Leandro while he bit back a curse after having been
snapped by a paparazzo.

'I thought you were enjoying the attention, *querida*,'
Leandro drawled with silken derision. 'You did dress to
attract it and hire a photographer to record the occasion.'

Molly breathed in so deep and long to control her
temper that she was vaguely surprised that she didn't
burst with the effort of holding her ire in. She did not
require his dislike of public attention to warn her that the
VIP lounge was not the place to start an argument with
a guy who wouldn't go down without a very aggressive
fight. Biding her time, she clenched her small white
teeth together until they had boarded his private jet. Even
while she was appreciating the sheer luxurious comfort
of the cabin, she was already wondering how sound-
proofed it would be as she didn't fancy their row providing entertainment for the air crew.

Layers of white organza foaming all around her, she
settled into a leather seat and did up the belt.

'Possibly asking you to keep the dress on wasn't a
good idea,' Leandro conceded soon after take-off.

'Oh, well, at least you didn't ask me to put a paper
bag over my head and pretend I didn't know you back
at the airport!' Molly snapped back.

An imperious ebony brow climbed. 'What is the
meaning of that strange comment?'

'That when you criticise me for hiring a photographer, you expose just how unreal your expectations are!' Molly extended, jerking open her seat belt to plunge upright again. 'This is supposed to be my wedding day. Unlike you, I haven't been there and done it before and I would have enjoyed a more memorable occasion. Of course, what I might want doesn't matter in the least to you...you're not just naturally authoritative, Leandro—you're well on the way to being a domineering tyrant!'

'You're hysterical,' Leandro informed her coldly.

'No, I'm not. If I was hysterical I would be throwing things and screaming. As it is, I'm just furious with you. Of course I wanted photos of my wedding! Some pretence that this was a normal marriage may come in useful in the future. Or would you be happy to tell our child that we have no photos because it was a shotgun wedding and you didn't see the need to dignify or celebrate the occasion in the usual way?'

Simmering dark golden eyes lit on her with punitive force. 'If you had wanted a photographer you should have mentioned it to me—'

'When? You were abroad and I wasn't allowed to have anything to do with the arrangements,' she reminded him.

'I assumed you'd be relieved to have everything taken care of for you,' Leandro retorted with cool assurance.

'What was wrong with asking me how I felt about it? But then you don't ask me anything, do you?' Molly sniped. 'You don't care how I feel, so why would you bother?'

'If I didn't care about you, you wouldn't have that

ring on your finger,' Leandro shot back at her with deflating conviction.

'No, if you cared you wouldn't have threatened me to ensure you *got* that ring on my finger!' Molly traded without skipping a beat. 'That was the act of a very ruthless guy, who doesn't care what he has to do to get what he wants.'

Smouldering dark golden eyes collided with hers in direct challenge. 'I regard it as a necessary act, driven by my understandable concern for your welfare—an action which ensured that I am now in the perfect position to look after you and my unborn child. Right now, I see that role as my primary purpose in life.'

Her cheeks hectically flushed and her eyes bright with indignation, Molly wanted to jump up and down with thwarted rage. He wasn't yielding a shamefaced inch to her perfectly reasonable complaints. Even worse, he was justifying his behaviour without a blush. How was she supposed to argue with a guy who wouldn't roll over and play dead for even twenty seconds? Worse still, a guy who clearly genuinely thought she couldn't cope without him.

'You don't know *how* to have a relationship, do you?' Molly accused next, one hand fiercely gripping the back of a seat to stay steady as air turbulence buffeted the plane. 'Instead of trying to win my trust and appreciation, you used threats. Maybe aggression works well in business, but you can't forge healthy relationships with human beings that way.'

Watching her sway, Leandro strode forward and swept her right off her feet and up into his arms. He supposed she would see that as aggressive as well, but if she didn't have enough sense to sit down or at least remove her ridiculously high and unstable shoes, he had no plans to wait until she fell and hurt herself.

'Put me down, Leandro!' Molly shouted at him, all fear of being overheard by the air crew overpowered by that very unwelcome demonstration of superior strength.

Leandro elbowed open the door of the sleeping compartment and lowered her with exaggerated gentleness down onto the bed. He sank down on its edge and flipped off her high heels with confident hands. 'You're my wife now. Of course I care about you. We will be celebrating our marriage with a very large and stylish party at my home tomorrow evening, *gatita*.'

Tumbled back against the pillows, her black curls rumpled, Molly opened her green eyes very wide at that announcement. Her wounded feelings were instantly soothed by the idea that he was willing to show her off as a wife at a big party. Such an act would, in some measure, make up for the disappointing wedding he had subjected her to. 'You should have told me that sooner.'

'I don't like parties much more than I like weddings,' Leandro confided.

Locked in connection with his heavily lashed dark eyes, Molly was finding it a challenge to breathe. He had a lot of faults, but he was gorgeous to look at, she conceded abstractedly, the hum of his magnetic attraction pulsing through her like a wake-up call and stealing what remained of her annoyance. Her fingers closed over the tip of his silk tie to tug him down to her. 'You're a lost cause. You don't tell your wife something like that on your wedding day,' she sighed.

'Was it that bad?' he queried in sincere surprise.

'Yes, but you're going to make it better,' Molly

muttered, one slender hand curving over a hard, muscular thigh.

Leandro was enthralled by the covetous look in her expressive eyes, the hunger she just couldn't hide. It set alight a desire that only ever ignited in her radius. He pressed her back against the pillows and captured her pouting pink lips with the intoxicating urgency of his, parting them with a stroke of his wicked tongue and delving deep with a provocation that made her gasp beneath the onslaught and shiver.

Molly surfaced to the discovery that her corset top and bra were being deftly unhooked. She felt limp on the outside and hot as hell on the inside. The little responsive quivers still lingering in intimate places swiftly expanded into wholehearted pleasure when he cupped the warm weight of her bare breasts and his thumbs rubbed the protruding pink points of her nipples. The stiff, swollen peaks were tormentingly sensitive and the feel of his mouth on the throbbing crests soon wrenched a moan from her throat while her hips writhed in helpless reaction.

'I love your breasts, *querida*,' Leandro husked, lingering over the creamy swells to ensure that he wrung the utmost enjoyment from her responsive body.

She was twisting under him when he dragged his appreciative mouth from a lush wet bud and dispensed with her flowing skirt. He sprang off the bed to remove his jacket and tie. As he peeled off his shirt Leandro feasted his masculine gaze appreciatively on his bride's bewitching appearance in delicate white panties and lace stockings. All of a sudden he was willing to concede that marriage could have definite compensations.

'You look fantastically sexy,' he told her in a roughened undertone. 'I can't take my eyes off you.'

Molly was suffering from a similar problem. The golden-skinned physique he was revealing as he stripped was drop-dead gorgeous, from his well-defined pec and ab muscles to his narrow hips and long, strong thighs. Her admiring appraisal sank to the potent erection visible below his clinging boxers. A tight feeling knotted deep in her pelvis and a surge of answering heat washed up through her. Embarrassed by her susceptibility to his spectacular dark good looks, she focused on her bare toes instead. The strength of her passion for him shocked her.

When he came down on the bed beside her she closed her arms round him, loving the scent of his skin and the warm, hair-roughened feel of him against her own softer skin. She wasn't going to fall in love with him, though, she warned herself. She was darned if she would give him more than he was prepared to offer her. He extracted her from her remaining garments and slowly worked his erotic way down over her squirming body, giving her pleasure with his every caress. The tense sensation at the swollen heart of her was like a sweet pain that kept on twisting tighter and tighter while her squirming hips dug into the mattress beneath her, blindly seeking the satisfaction he withheld.

His hair brushed her stomach, his tongue dipping to swirl round the shallow indentation of her navel before progressing to a more intimate destination between her slender thighs. She went rigid with surprise, but he was persuasive and her body was too hot for her to resist. The wild, fierce longing inside her had neither conscience nor shame. Wherever he touched she burned, her heart thumping frantically fast in receipt of the exquisite delight of his exploration. She didn't recognise herself in that storm of excitement that drove her out of control and left her helpless in the spellbinding hold of his caresses. A single forefinger probed her tight delicate entrance and she cried out and bucked, feverishly ready for him.

'*Dios mio, querida...* I can't wait,' Leandro confessed in a throaty growl of impatience.

Her excitement was at an unbearable height when he pulled her to him and began to push into her wet, silky depths. The pleasure was so intense for her that she cried out. He stole the sound with his mouth. And then he was moving, driving his thick, virile shaft into her, satisfying the hollow ache that had tormented her with the energising force and rhythm of his masculine need. She rocked up to receive him and he pushed a hand below her bottom to hold her there while he ground into her with ravenous hunger.

'Nothing has *ever* felt this good,' Leandro groaned with earthy satisfaction, scorching golden eyes welded to her as he took and gave pleasure, a faint sheen of sweat dampening his lean, bronzed face.

The waves of excitement came closer and closer together until her awareness exploded into a world of searing light and ecstatic sensation. Her whole body clenched in the melting throes of her climax and he shuddered over her and thrust deeper still so that the rapturous tremors quivering through her went on and on and left her drowning in hot, sweet pleasure.

'Hmm.' Leandro growled, rolling back on the pillows and lifting her over him. 'In bed you're absolute perfection,' he confided in a tone thick with male satisfaction.

Her arms easing round him while she revelled in the kisses he was stringing across her brow, Molly wondered how she really felt about that particular compliment. She supposed sex was the true single source of her attraction and, whether she liked it or not, a very important component in the future success of their marriage. She supposed it was unrealistic and greedy for her to want more than that from a guy who she felt was rather out of her league when it came to looks and success.

'I'd like to stay here for hours, but it won't be long until we land. A helicopter will fly us to the castle, where I know my family will be waiting to meet you,' Leandro advanced without any audible enthusiasm.

Molly's head shot up, tousled black curls almost standing on end. 'What castle?' she gasped.

'My home.'

'You live in a...*castle*?' Molly prompted in a panic. 'And I'm going to meet your family *immediately*?'

Leandro watched in astonishment as his bride leapt free of him and off the bed. 'What's wrong?'

'Look at me!' she launched at him in dismay as she caught her reflection in a mirrored wardrobe. 'I'm a mess and what am I going to wear?'

'Your cases are here—'

'But I don't know what to wear in a castle.' Molly studied him with fierce resentment, because she hated the feeling that she was out of her depth and the casually proffered news that he lived in a castle had driven that fact home hard enough to hurt.

Still stark naked, she threw herself at one of the cases and tried to haul it off the floor.

'What are you doing?' Leandro sprang up to snatch

the suitcase off her and lift it on to the bed. 'Don't try to lift anything that heavy.'

On her knees on the carpet, she was fumbling for her keys in the little Dorothy bag she had carried to the church. Leandro draped his shirt over her shoulders, where it hung like a tent round her tiny frame.

'What am I going to wear?' she gasped strickenly, rooting with desperate hands through a pile of casual garments in bright colours. 'I don't have anything fancy.'

'I sent you shopping,' Leandro reminded her, as if he could not credit the idea that a woman might not take the fullest possible advantage of such an opportunity.

'But I didn't buy much because I'm pregnant,' she told him in frustration. 'In a few weeks nothing normal-sized will fit me and I'll have to buy maternity stuff, so I decided not to waste money.'

'It doesn't matter what you wear,' Leandro said in an attempt to calm her down.

Molly selected a cerise and black polka dot summer dress. 'Would this do?'

'Whatever you wear will be fine. You're my wife and you don't have anyone to impress within our home.'

Molly was touched by that assurance, but he had been born to life in a castle and she was apprehensive about meeting his family and did not want to make a bad first impression. 'It's not that simple.'

Leandro closed firm hands over her restless ones to force her to look up at him. 'It *is*.'

When she redid her make-up, she thought that her flat-tened, somewhat messy curls and swollen mouth were dead giveaways to the fact that she might just have got out of bed with her husband. Her dress was very casual and in no way impressive. Before they boarded the helicopter she studied Leandro in the act of turning his handsome face up in welcome to the heat of the Spanish sunshine. Well-cut black silk hair in faultless order, he looked infuriatingly immaculate in appearance.

And even though she had told herself that she was prepared for a castle, she was certainly not in any way prepared for the vast building that filled her view as the helicopter swooped in low to land. Leandro's castle was the genuine article, complete with turrets, towers and medieval walls. It sat on a hill surrounded by extensive landscaped gardens and overlooked a fertile valley covered with woods and olive groves.

'No wonder you think the sun rises and sets on you,' Molly breathed, no longer marvelling at the level of his self-assurance. 'Who on earth are all those people waiting at the entrance?'

'Our staff. Our marriage is a major event for the household and everyone will want to welcome you to your new home and wish you well.'

Molly was convinced that she could only be a disappointment. Conscious of the barrage of curious eyes nailed to her, she curled herself in by Leandro's side. 'They're all staring,' she hissed behind teeth arranged into a fixed smile.

'Probably because they think I robbed the cradle for you,' Leandro breathed wryly.

But that was the least of the hurdles Molly was about to face. A few steps in through the very grand entrance hall hung with giant paintings and life-size pieces of marble sculpture, she was greeted by Leandro's mother, a tall, older woman with silvering dark hair and cold eyes. Wearing a formal suit, she was accompanied by two younger women, dressed rather like her clones. Introductions were performed and the atmosphere grew no warmer. Doña Maria and her daughters, Estefania and Julieta, simply stared woodenly at Molly while she struggled to voice friendly words of greeting and behave as though she hadn't noticed that anything was lacking in her welcome. Goodness, she certainly hoped they were not all going to be sharing the same roof.

Leandro was astonished when he strode into the crowded salon where a formal reception appeared to be in full swing. He saw faces he hadn't seen in ten or twenty years. His mother had assembled every relation they possessed right down to distant cousins to provide an intimidating line up for his bride.

'Is this the party you mentioned?' Molly whispered, feeling horrendously underdressed when she compared the other women's elegant formal wear and glittering jewellery to her own casual appearance.

'No, this is only the extended family circle. I'm sorry. I had no idea this was planned.'

Viewing the packed room, Molly swallowed hard, but tilted her chin. She had to ask, she simply *had* to. 'Does your mother live with you?'

'No, she bases herself in Seville these days and makes occasional visits.' Leandro rested an arm at her spine and guided her round to perform introductions. Many of the guests spoke English, but few had a strong enough grasp of the language for a relaxing conversation. Molly realised that if she intended to fit in, she needed to acquire a working knowledge of Spanish as quickly as possible.

'I have to learn Spanish fast,' she informed Leandro in a lull between the excruciatingly polite conversations. 'Obviously you're not always going to be around to act as my interpreter. Do you know anyone who would be willing to teach me?'

'I'll organise it. Learning even a little Spanish would make it easier for you to settle in.' Leandro looked down at her and smiled in appreciation. As his lean, darkly handsome face shed all cool and reserve she was spellbound by the change in him and her luminous green eyes locked to him.

His sister Julieta came up and said something to him. 'A phone call,' he told Molly. 'I'll try not to be long, *querida*.'

'*Dios mio!*' the pretty brunette murmured, treating Molly's absorbed face to an assessing appraisal and then laughing. 'The way you look at Leandro! You're actually in love with my brother.'

Hot colour drenched Molly's cheeks and she was about to argue with that statement when it occurred to her that, as Leandro's bride, it might be wiser for her to keep quiet on that score. Was there some particular way she looked at him? Embarrassment claimed her.

Away from her intimidating mother, Julieta was a different girl. She lifted two glasses from a passing tray and offered one to Molly with a friendly smile.

'I can't drink,' Molly responded with an apologetic grimace.

'Sorry…I forgot you were preggers,' the attractive brunette confided in perfect colloquial English. 'We're all still in shock about that. It took you five minutes to achieve what Aloise couldn't manage in five *years*!'

That one illuminating sentence satisfied Molly's curiosity on several scores. Her husband's first marriage had lasted five years and his wife, Aloise, had failed to conceive. Did that history explain why Leandro had been so convinced that Molly wouldn't fall pregnant? She rather thought it did.

'Come and meet Fernando,' Julieta urged, tugging at her elbow. 'He's younger and more fun.'

Fernando Santos was the estate manager and a handsome athletic young man in his late twenties. Julieta got very giggly and juvenile with him and the couple exchanged jokes, until Doña Maria sternly beckoned her daughter back to her side from the other side of the room.

'Are you the person I should ask if there is a vacant shed I could use to house a pottery kiln?' Molly enquired hopefully, glancing in Leandro's direction and wondering why her husband was staring fixedly at her just at that moment.

'Yes, Your Excellency. There may well be a suitable building in the old farmyard,' Fernando replied. 'We had to build new sheds for the agricultural machinery and several are now vacant.'

'Call me Molly,' Molly suggested. A sunny smile of satisfaction wreathed her animated features at the knowledge that there was no longer a day job preventing her from fulfilling her artistic ambitions and doing what she really wanted to do with her time.

Brown eyes resting admiringly on her vivacious face, Fernando gave her an apologetic look. 'That would cause offence to your new family. You're the duke's wife and the traditional formalities are carefully upheld on the estate.'

'It's going to take some getting used to,' Molly sighed.

'But I can speak for the whole staff when I tell you that we are all pleased that His Excellency has remarried,' the young Spaniard told her warmly.

Leandro joined them at that point and Fernando became conspicuously less chatty. Leandro seemed very cool and distant. Following a conversation about the olive groves, carried out in English apparently for her benefit, Leandro walked her out onto the spacious landing. Molly glanced up at him and then stiffened, forewarned by the black ice chill of his dark gaze and the forbidding tension of his lean, powerful face that something was wrong.

'Keep your distance from Fernando Santos,' Leandro breathed with cutting cool. 'Although he is an exemplary employee, he has a sleazy reputation with women and it will do you no good to be seen to enjoy his company to such an extent.'

Thoroughly taken aback by that unexpected rebuke, Molly said, 'What on earth are you trying to suggest?'

'That you don't flirt with him and do maintain a formal distance with him when you meet.'

Furious resentment snaked through Molly's tense figure. 'I wasn't flirting. For goodness' sake, we were only talking for a few minutes,' she protested in a vehement undertone. 'I didn't have you picked as the jealous type, but thanks for the warning!'

Equally taken aback by that wrathful retaliation, Leandro froze. Aggrieved gold flashed into his intent gaze. 'I have never been jealous in my life,' he asserted with freezing dignity. 'But your behaviour was attracting attention—'

'On my *wedding* day? When I'm carrying your child? Is it everyone round here who's crazy or just you?' Molly raised a disbelieving brow and stalked away from him in high dudgeon.

A shudder of steely self-restraint raked through

Leandro's big, powerful frame. She was a tiny figure in a bright dress that clung to her firm, rounded curves at breast and hip and skimmed slender thighs that led down into flawless legs. His teeth gritted. He resisted the urge to drag her back and make her listen to him. She liked male company and men liked her. He knew how close she was to Jez Andrews. Her best friend was a man, not a woman, and he was not comfortable with that fact. Another man might easily misinterpret her easy smiles and friendliness as an invitation. She also seemed blissfully unaware of how very sexy she was even in that polka-dot dress, which looked as though it would be more at home on a beach…

CHAPTER SEVEN

THE following morning, Molly knocked on the communicating door in her bedroom and waited, shifting off one foot onto the other. When there was no answer she opened it and she saw yet another terrifyingly imposing bedroom containing huge ornate furniture that looked as if it had been designed a good few centuries ago. It seemed all the more intimidating when set against its backdrop of gilded paneled walls. She breathed in deep. Maybe she should have been prepared for Leandro's absence, she told herself ruefully.

After all, she had slept alone. Alone on her wedding night. While it was true that they had consummated their marriage on board his jet, she had not expected to be left by herself. But then she had not expected separate bedroom suites either, had she? Last night she had drifted off to sleep while she waited for him in solitary splendour. A maid had awoken her with breakfast in bed. It was only while she was getting dressed and chose to investigate further that the truth finally sank in on her: the dressing-room closets contained only her clothes and a door in her vast bedroom connected with his.

A knock sounded on her bedroom door and Julieta walked in. 'Oh, good, you're up. Leandro has asked me to take you shopping for a dress for the party tonight—'

'Where is he?' Molly asked.

His sister looked surprised by the question. 'At the bank, of course.'

Married one day, back to work the next, Molly reflected. Her soft mouth tightened because she refused to give way to the feeling that he had abandoned her. After all, she wasn't a child and she might be in a strange environment, but she would soon get used to it. She would manage fine without him. By the looks of it, she didn't have much choice.

Julieta chattered all the way downstairs about where they were going to go shopping, while Molly scanned her lavish surroundings with all the apprehension of an ordinary person suddenly waking up to find themselves lost in a royal palace. But the instant her insecurity was ready to rise, she crushed it flat and refused to acknowledge those feelings. Leandro's castle was where she was going to bring her baby up and the last thing her child needed was a mother who lacked self-esteem. As they reached the foot of the stairs a middle-aged manservant addressed both women in Spanish.

'Basilio says that my mother would like a word with you before we go out,' Julieta translated, showing Molly into an elegant sitting room where Doña Maria awaited her.

'Molly…' The tall older woman greeted her with an acerbic smile. 'Leandro asked me to have a word with you about the household arrangements. He doesn't think you'll be up to taking charge immediately, so I agreed to continue the job until you feel able.'

Faced with that vote of no confidence from her bride-groom while at the same time wondering exactly what came under the heading of household arrangements, Molly felt cornered and cut off at the knees. 'Right,' she said uncertainly.

'Dealing with the staff and the catering for a house as large as this one is a complex task,' Doña Maria pointed out. 'Aloise had the benefit of growing up in a similar home and knew exactly what was required. Basilio is also an excellent major-domo. He has to be. Leandro expects the *castillo* to run like clockwork.'

With a bright smile that refused to betray an ounce of nervous tension, Molly lifted her chin. 'I'm sure I'll rise to the challenge. My experience in catering will help.'

'I'm impressed by your confidence.'

Fed up with the woman's subtle put-downs, Molly lifted her head high to say, 'I can understand that your son's sudden marriage has come as a shock to you and I have no wish to fall out with you. But this is my home now and I intend to adjust to the way of life here because I want our child to be happy—'

'But you will never be the wife whom Leandro needs! Aloise was the love of his life and irreplaceable. You will never belong here as she did. You can only be an embar-rassment to my son. *A waitress!*' the dowager duchesa exclaimed with a contemptuous sound of disgust. 'I *know* that you threw yourself at Leandro from the first moment you saw him—'

'Where on earth did you get that idea from?' Molly cut in, anger betraying her determination to stay firmly in control whatever the provocation.

'Krystal Forfar is one of my oldest friends. She witnessed your first meeting with Leandro and saw you for what you are—a scheming, gold-digging little tramp!'

Cut to the bone by the older woman's abuse, Molly was rigid. 'I gather you're the anonymous party behind the financial offer that was made to me.'

'I don't know what you're talking about,' Doña Maria proclaimed, her stare unflinching.

But Molly was convinced she had found the culprit and saw no point in further dispute. Having decided to reject her son's bride sight unseen, Doña Maria was all the more bitter for being forced to accept her as a daughter-in-law.

'I would advise you not to make false allegations against me,' the older woman continued. 'Leandro would never forgive you.'

Ten minutes later, comfortably enclosed in a chauffeur-driven limousine with Julieta, Molly was considering the likely outcome of tackling Leandro about her mother-in-law. Of course, how could she prove anything? She had no documentary evidence to show and no witnesses of what had been said to her. And did she really need to run to Leandro to tell tales barely thirty-six hours into their marriage? Surely she could cope better than that? *The love of his life*, however, had a fine ring to it and she knew it would be a long time, if ever, before she forgot that description of Aloise.

'Was your mother very fond of Aloise?' Molly asked Leandro's sister.

The pretty brunette flushed and failed to meet her eyes. 'Mama knew Aloise when she was a child. We all did. She lived only a few miles away and our families were close. Her death shattered us all. The accident was very sudden and truly tragic. Aloise had so much to live for. Everyone admired her.'

By the sound of it, Leandro had selected the perfect wife. A childhood friend and neighbour, popular with his family and with whom he had shared a great deal more than he could ever share with Molly. She was also willing to bet that he had taken the love of his life away on a honeymoon.

The dress was a vibrant emerald green that gave her skin a glow of creamy perfection and highlighted her bright eyes. The glistening fabric shaped her body from bust to hip and flared out into a short skirt.

'You will turn every head in the room, *gatita*,' Leandro forecast from behind her.

Surprise made Molly jump and she spun round from her inspection of the mirror. 'I didn't know you were back.'

'I'm sorry I missed dinner. Work had piled up while I was in London. I won't be long. All I have to do is shower and change.' Brilliant dark golden eyes rested on her and her tummy flipped a somersault and her mouth ran dry. Sleek and dark in an elegant business suit with his black hair slightly ruffled and a blue-black shadow of stubble defining his hard, handsome jaw line, he looked utterly spectacular to her appreciative gaze. 'But I thought you might want to wear these this evening…'

He extended a jewellery case.

Molly lifted the lid to reveal a magnificent necklace composed of perfectly matched large lustrous pearls and matching drop earrings. 'These are amazing.'

'There's a tremendous collection of jewellery in the safe, all of which is now yours to wear.'

Molly lifted out the pearl necklace. He helped her

attach the diamond-studded clasp, his fingertips brushing the nape of her neck. She put on the earrings. Worn together, the set looked incredibly opulent. 'How old are the pieces?'

'Turn of the last century, given on the occasion of my great-grandfather's birth…

'And this is from me…' Leandro extended a much smaller box.

Her heart beating very fast, Molly opened it and studied the glittering diamond ring with stunned eyes. 'It's gorgeous.'

Leandro extracted the ring and reached for her hand to slide the ring onto the same finger as her wedding band. 'We missed out on the usual steps, *querida*.'

'I love it.' And when she collided with his shimmering dark eyes she suspected that some day she might well start loving him too, for sometimes he could do or say something that cut right to the heart of her concerns and touched her deep. The night they had met he had told her that she made him feel more alive than he had felt in years and he had called that a cause for celebration. In the same way the giving of the equivalent of an engagement ring and the recognition that their relationship had skipped several important stages made her eyes prickle with stinging tears of appreciation. 'I really love it…'

'I'd better get in that shower.' Leandro strode back to the door between their bedrooms and a moment later he was gone.

She admired her new collection of jewellery and enjoyed the fact that he obviously wanted her to be able to hold her own amongst the other women at the party.

'So how long have the separate bedrooms for husband

and wife been operating?' Molly enquired when they were descending the magnificent staircase together.

Leandro dealt her a look of surprise. 'Centuries.'

Molly leant closer and whispered huskily, 'Time for a change.'

The familiar citrus-fresh scent of her hair flared his nostrils and heated his appreciative dark gaze. 'You could be right, *querida*.'

'Is that you actually admitting that you might be wrong about something?'

'No, that's you misinterpreting me,' Leandro quipped without skipping a beat.

Knots of guests in elegant dinner jackets and exquisite gowns and glittering jewellery drifted into the beautifully decorated ballroom to greet them. As the evening wore on Molly's head swam with the sheer number of different names and faces she tried to match. She met Leandro's neighbours, friends and loads of other bankers. It was a warm evening and the crush of people and the noise of the music and the chattering voices combined in a suffocating wave that made her feel slightly nauseous and dizzy. She drifted over to the doors that stood open onto the terrace to allow fresh air to filter in. Just as she was hanging back from joining Leandro, who was patently talking business with a group of like-minded serious men, Julieta approached her. Looping her arm round Molly's to draw her into a girlie aside, Julieta whispered, 'Can I trust you with a secret?'

'If you want to,' Molly responded a little uncertainly.

'I've been seeing Fernando Santos for weeks,' Leandro's youngest sister confided in an explosive rush. 'I'm crazy about him!'

'My goodness…' Molly was taken aback by that confession and not quite sure she wanted the responsibility of it. It had not taken her long to work out that, while Julieta was warm-hearted and likeable, she was also impulsive and immature for a girl of twenty-one.

Julieta gave her a warning look. 'If the truth were to come out, my family would break us up and Fernando would lose his job, so please don't tell anyone.'

Molly nodded and hoped that Leandro was wrong in his conviction that the handsome estate manager was a womaniser. More streetwise than the Spanish girl had ever had to be, Molly paid more heed to Fernando when he came over to speak to her. He startled her by bowing over her hand and kissing it. That gesture along with his ready smile and conversation showed him to be a man who was very much at home in female company and prided himself on the fact.

'I've identified a couple of buildings that might be suitable for your purpose, Your Excellency. Would you prefer me to discuss this with your husband?' he asked.

'No, I'll deal with it. My husband is a busy man,' Molly countered.

'I'll let you know, then, when the sheds are ready for inspection,' Fernando told her, tensing as Julieta sent him a flirtatious smile and then looking away with an unease that did not bode well for the relationship. Perhaps he should have thought of the risks before getting involved, Molly thought, all her concern reserved for Julieta, whom she could see was in deep enough to get badly hurt. Perspiration beading her short upper lip, Molly suddenly sucked in a deep breath, striving to counter the sickening light-headed sensation overcoming her.

'Are you feeling all right?' Fernando asked Molly abruptly. 'You've turned very pale.'

'I'm fine,' Molly lied, hurriedly turning away to find somewhere to sit down. But that quick movement was too much and a wave of dizziness drenched her in a cold sweat of discomfort. With a gasp, she swayed and began to fall. A split second before she hit the floor with a crash, someone grabbed her.

When she recovered consciousness, she was in another room and Leandro was standing over her where she lay on a sofa and studying her with stark concern etched in his lean bronzed features. A middle-aged stranger was taking her pulse and viewing her with a frown while Leandro introduced him as the family doctor, Edmundo Mendoza.

'You should be taking more rest at this time, Your Excellency,' he censured.

'I just felt dizzy. It was so warm and airless.'

'You're not used to the climate yet and in a few short weeks it will be much warmer,' Dr Mendoza warned her. 'Give yourself time to acclimatise.'

'I should have ensured that you sat down,' Leandro groaned.

'I was just a little faint,' Molly said dismissively.

'But suppose that faint had occurred on the stairs,' the doctor urged, clearly a man who liked to visualise worst-case scenarios.

'You should rest now. Our guests will understand,' Leandro declared.

'I don't need to be treated like an invalid,' Molly muttered while she wondered if absolutely everybody present was already aware that she was a pregnant bride. She cringed at the idea.

Leandro, all macho-managing-male at that instant, scooped her up off the sofa. 'What were you talking about with Santos? At first I thought he had said something to upset you when you turned away from him. I was coming to join you and just got there in time to catch you before you hit the floor—'

Surprised that Leandro had been watching her that closely, Molly explained her need for a place to house a kiln.

'Why on earth didn't you ask me to deal with that?' he demanded.

'I didn't want to bother you and…I like doing things for myself,' Molly admitted.

'Possibly I'm going out on a limb here,' Leandro breathed tautly, 'but right now when you're pregnant doesn't seem the wisest time to be messing around with kilns and clay—'

'Don't be silly!' Molly snapped, furious at that suggestion. 'It's not heavy work—'

'I'm not artistic, but neither am I stupid.' Leandro's expressive mouth compressed. 'Loading and unloading a kiln must be arduous—however, if you were prepared to have one of the estate workers helping you with the more demanding tasks, I would have no objection.'

'Okay,' Molly conceded to that arrangement with reluctance as he laid her down on the bed and took off her shoes for her. 'But I need my own corner to work in. Will your family mind me being a potter?'

Leandro paused at the door. 'It's none of their business.'

Some of Molly's tension ebbed at that reassuringly independent response. 'Your mother and eldest sister don't like me.'

'Give them the time to get to know you,' Leandro

advised. 'You don't have much experience of how families operate, do you?'

Molly stiffened defensively. 'I lived in a family for the first nine years of my life—before my mother died and my grandmother gave me up for adoption,' she explained when he frowned in surprise. 'There was me, my mother and my older sister…except my sister was more like my mother because she's the only person I can remember looking after me when I was very young—'

'I forgot that you had a sister. Where is she now?'

'I don't know. I sort of closed the door on that bit of my life and I'm not sure I would want to open it again,' she confided, thinking of the hurt she still felt at that rejection and the wrenching sense of loss she had suffered for years afterwards.

'I'll call your maid to help you get ready for bed,' Leandro murmured.

'You're sleeping here tonight,' Molly reminded him and then flushed to the roots of her hair at her nerve in making that reminder.

Leandro had come to a sudden halt. He looked back at her with brilliant dark heavily lashed eyes that made her heart thump and a slow, sensual smile curved his handsome mouth. Her desire for him never failed to excite him. He would be responsible, though, he told himself equally forcefully; he would check that angle out with the doctor first. He needed to take better care of her. It galled him that she should have gone to Fernando Santos for help sooner than ask her husband for it.

Molly dozed off soon after she got into bed and wakened only when Leandro came into the room. 'It's all right—I'm awake,' she announced when she registered that he was trying to move around quietly.

Leandro studied her in the lamplight. Her black curls fell in a dense cloud round her narrow shoulders, framing her piquant face and vivid green eyes. His desire was instantaneous and just an upgrade of the simmering need that had purred in the background of his awareness all day. No matter where he was or what he was doing, he stayed hot and hungry for her.

Molly watched him undress. Indeed she luxuriated in that intimacy and hoped that the separate-bedroom concept of living would now die a natural death, for it would not be easy for them to enjoy private moments as a couple in a household so filled with other people. Yet more than anything else they needed that time and privacy. *The love of his life*; oh, how those words were set to haunt her and disrupt her peace! But when she saw Leandro in all his naked bronzed magnificence, her thoughts became far more primitive. He had a professional athlete's hard, sculpted contours of power and rippling muscle. The bold jut of his erect sex induced a melting liquid sensation low in her pelvis.

'You want me, *querida*,' Leandro husked, settling hot golden eyes of appreciation on her and coming down on the bed beside her.

'Yes…' Her soft pink lips parted on a whisper of sound because her heart was thumping like an express train at full tilt and she could hardly breathe for anticipation.

He took her hand and encouraged her to touch him and the hammer of her heartbeat only got louder when she stroked his rigid shaft. Moist heat blossomed in answer between her thighs. He drove her lips apart with hungry urgency and she fell back against the pillows while he extracted her from her nightdress. The plunge of his tongue made her shiver convulsively. He explored the soft, firm swell of her breasts and tugged on the tender pink crests until she was moaning and shifting her hips up to him.

Molly could feel herself going out of control very fast. It was as if all the nervous constraints of the day were suddenly being torn from her and every craving were being channelled into one piercing need. She wanted him, she really, *really* wanted him with an intensity she couldn't hide. His exploration of the slick pink cleft at the heart of her drove her insane with delight.

'You feel like hot silk, *gatita*,' Leandro growled, tipping her leg back to rise over her, impatient to ease the painful ache of his arousal.

He sank into her willing body and she loosed a wanton moan of pleasure. Her excitement climbed with every powerful thrust. The raw pulse of hunger throbbing through her responsive flesh, she arched up to take him deeper. A wild cry of satisfaction escaped her as orgasm took her to the dizzy heights of intolerable pleasure and dropped her back down to mortal earth again.

'Did I live up to your expectations, *querida*?' Leandro asked teasingly, skimming long brown fingers through her mane of hair where it lay across the pillows, his attention welded to her hectically flushed smiling face. 'You surpassed them,' Molly whispered truthfully, her arms wrapping round his lean. strong frame.

Dimly she grasped that at such moments Leandro felt very much as if he was hers and she felt infinitely more close to him. Sex as a substitute for love, well, why not? she asked herself irritably. It was surely a lot safer than signing up for the kind of love slavery that had wrecked her natural mother, Cathy's ability to be content. She could be happy. She *would* be happy. A man who had married her for the sake of their child took marriage seriously and would make every effort to help her adjust to her new life.

But when Molly wakened the next day in an empty bed and fled at speed across the bedroom to check the room next door, she was no longer quite so confident. Leandro had already left. Yet it was the weekend. Couldn't he have taken time off to be with her for even one day? Or was she expecting too much? What was he telling her about his priorities? And her level of importance in his life…?

CHAPTER EIGHT

MOLLY glanced out the open doors of her studio when she heard a car enter the courtyard. It was Julieta, who came home from Seville on Fridays to see Fernando, who lived on the estate. She always parked her car in the courtyard well away from his house in the hope of defeating the gossips. Molly looked away again, minding her own business, but wishing she didn't know as much as she did about the relationship. Common sense told her that Leandro would be outraged that his sister was involved in so blatant an affair with his employee.

Preferring not to dwell on a situation that was outside her control, Molly studied the shelves of gleaming pottery against the opposite wall with a warm sense of accomplishment. She had been experimenting with a new glaze and a wood-fired kiln and was delighted with the results. In the months that had elapsed since her marriage, she had worked hard. Fernando Santos had given her very useful assistance when she had decided to set up a small pottery in the old farmyard. Her kiln was housed next door in a fire-proofed shed and organising a proper studio had been the natural next step.

She gazed out the glass doors at the orchards and the blue, blue sky above. She had a wonderful working environment and plenty of free time to devote to her potter's art. So why wasn't she happy?

She could see her reflection in the glass doors and even the large heavy-duty apron she wore could not conceal her new fecund shape. Her boyish slenderness had vanished as her pregnancy advanced. She was six months along now and her pregnant tummy was a firm and protuberant little mound and even her breasts had expanded enough to make her feel top-heavy. She had worried that as her waist ebbed Leandro would find her less attractive. But that had proved a needless concern. Leandro had embraced every change in her body with masculine enthusiasm.

Yes, indeed, Molly reflected wryly. In fact in the sex department her every want was more than satisfied. No complaints there. Leandro slept with her every night and he was a very lusty guy. But somewhere along the line, maybe when she woke up alone or spent yet another solitary evening while he worked late or travelled abroad, the sizzling passion that she shared with her husband had begun to remind her more of what they *didn't* have than what they did. She had wardrobes full of designer clothes and a fantastic collection of jewellery. When he remembered her existence Leandro bought her beautiful gifts like the platinum watch on her wrist or the array of perfumes from which she now had to choose.

Unhappily, she was convinced that, while Leandro was rarely out of her thoughts, Leandro himself didn't remember his wife's existence very often. It would never occur to him to phone her when he was away from her. He would never confide his deepest thoughts in her, nor would he even answer her curious questions about Aloise. Indeed he had labelled her curiosity about his first wife 'unhealthy' and had ensured that she was very reluctant to raise the topic again.

'I think you should tell Leandro to take a running jump and come home to London,' Jez had told Molly on the phone the night before. 'You're bored, you're lonely and you're in a foreign country. By the sounds of it, you see so little of your healthy duke that you might as well move back here. He could visit the kid when he comes over on business. At least you'd have a life in London.'

'I've never been a quitter. I don't want a divorce and a broken home for my child,' she argued vehemently. 'Marriage is for the long haul.'

'Your long haul, not his. You seem to be the one making all the sacrifices,' her best friend opined.

And wasn't that the truth? Molly thought ruefully. Marriage appeared to have made very little impression on either Leandro's schedule or his attitude to her. Leandro was strong, arrogant and reserved. She loved his strength, but hated being kept at arm's length. He shut her out and she desperately wanted to be let in so that she could get close to him somewhere other than in the bedroom. She had nobody but Julieta to talk to, and during the week Leandro's sister lived in Seville where she was studying fashion design. While Molly's regular Spanish lessons with a local teacher had led to a steady improvement in her grasp of the language, it was still an uphill challenge for her to have a decent chat with anyone. At least, however, she could now make herself understood with the castle staff. For the first couple of months, while she was unable to express the most basic requests, she had felt very inadequate and isolated.

Furthermore, her mother-in-law, far from basing herself as promised in Seville, remained firmly in residence below the same roof. Doña Maria froze Molly out in company and made little acid comments and digs under cover of polite conversation. That was one reason why Molly spent the greater part of her day in her studio, which Leandro had yet to even visit. He had promised to come but never quite made it. In much the same way he had not found the time to take any interest in the nursery being decorated for their unborn child.

A knock on the door shot Molly back to the present and she spun round to see Julieta, gorgeous in white shorts and T-shirt, smiling hopefully across the studio at her.

'It's my birthday tomorrow,' Julieta reminded her. 'Will you come up to town and go clubbing with me and my friends in the evening? You can stay the night at my place.'

It was on the tip of Molly's tongue to say no because she knew that Leandro would not approve. But then when did Leandro ever take her out anywhere? She was married to a workaholic too busy to waste his precious time entertaining his wife. Sudden defiance blazed through Molly. Since when had she been the sort of girl who sat home and did as she was told? On that thought, she accepted the invitation and Julieta was ecstatic at the prospect of introducing Molly to all her friends, for the two women had formed an increasingly close friendship, united by the truth that neither of them was capable of winning Doña Maria's approval. Nothing poor Julieta wore or indeed did got her critical mother's vote of confidence.

Late afternoon, Molly drove back to the *castillo* in

one of the estate Land Rovers that she had acquired for
her own use. Basilio knew her routine and he was sta-
tioned at the side door in the garden she always used to
avoid her mother-in-law, who sat in the grand salon off
the hall at that time of day. He swept open the door and
bowed low with a throbbing air of exaggerated respect
that very nearly provoked Molly into giggles.

'*Muchas gracias, Basilio*,' she said punctiliously,
touched by his unfailing efforts to give her the aristocratic airs she so conspicuously lacked.

She grabbed a magazine from the pile in her
bedroom and went off to luxuriate in a long bath.
Anticipation at the prospect of soon enjoying lively
company had brightened her eyes. She was already
planning to get her hair and nails done for her night out
on the town the following day. She wondered what she
would wear, reflecting that pregnant clubbers weren't
exactly cool or fashionable, and mentally flipped
through her extensive wardrobe for an outfit that would
magically conceal her rotund contours. So Leandro
wouldn't like it. Well, Leandro would have to roll with
the punches.

In the act of flipping through the glossy fashion
magazine for something to catch her interest, Molly
froze at the fleeting glimpse of a woman's face. Sitting
up in an abrupt movement, displaced water swilling
noisily all around her, Molly flipped back frantically
through the issue to find the relevant page while struggling to keep it dry at the same time.

Her heart skipped a beat when she finally relo-
cated the photograph of a very beautiful blonde woman
standing in a walled garden full of colourful flowers.
It was her sister, Ophelia, she was sure it was! Barely

able to breathe for excitement, Molly settled back to read the article. Ophelia was married now—well why not? Her sister was seven years older and a mother as well, Molly registered in growing astonishment. My goodness, Ophelia had already had three kids by a Greek businessman called Lysander Metaxis! Now why did that surname ring a familiar bell with her? Ophelia, who now evidently ran a plant nursery, had opened her home and garden in aid of a children's charity. Molly turned a page and stared fixedly at the picture of Madrigal Court. Her recognition of the lovely old Tudor house sent a cold shiver down her spine, rousing as it did unhappy memories.

She still remembered the initial excitement of first seeing that huge ancient house from her grandmother's car the day after her mother's funeral. She had been so hopelessly impressed that someone she was related to could possibly have enough money to live in a mansion. But her grandmother, Gladys, who could have given Doña Maria frostbite with her nasty tongue, had soon turned Molly's youthful excitement into a sick sense of apprehension. As soon as Gladys had returned from enrolling Ophelia in her new school, she had sat Molly down and told her that she couldn't possibly give her a permanent home.

'Your sister is sixteen. You're too young a child for me to take on,' her grandmother had told her.

Molly had fearfully sworn that she would be no trouble and that she would help out round the house and not get in the way, and the older woman had had to admit the true reasons why she wasn't prepared to raise her younger granddaughter.

'Your father was a foreigner and he already had a

wife when he got your mother pregnant with you. He was a loathsome man who jilted your mother at the altar long before you were born, but he still wouldn't let her alone to get on with her life!' Gladys Stewart had delivered with seething bitterness. 'It's a shameful disgrace for a woman to give birth to a child when she's not married, Molly, and that's why you can't live here with me. It'll be much better for all of us if you're adopted.'

Until today, she had never seen the big sister she adored, Molly recalled painfully. If a heart could be broken, hers had been smashed, as Ophelia had been the only stable loving influence in Molly's world since she was born. Her eyes wet from those recollections, Molly read on, eagerly sucking up every tiny personal detail about her sister's life. She hauled herself out of the bath and dried herself at frantic speed. She was going to get in touch with Ophelia. Why not? There was no mention of her grandmother in the article. She was only risking rejection and couldn't imagine the sister she remembered being that cruel. She was longing for another woman she could talk to, because it was impossible to admit the extent of her unhappiness to Julieta, and Jez was a man and didn't understand, for he simply urged her to walk out on her husband. As if that would be the easiest thing in the world to do!

Before she could lose her nerve, Molly flung on some clothes and went on the Internet in search of contact details for Ophelia. Madrigal Court had its own website and she sent an email to her sister, couched as casually as she could manage it, asking after the family parrot, Haddock, and including her mobile phone number. After all, Ophelia might not want to talk to her.

At that same moment, Leandro was in his office at the bank in Seville and sustaining a very taxing visit from an elderly uncle who professed to be very much shocked and disturbed by recent outrageous gossip on the estate relating to a family member's behaviour with an unnamed man. By the time all the complex and deeply apologetic and defensive outpourings had been waded through, Leandro was not a great deal wiser to the facts than he had been at the outset. His uncle, an old bachelor, had a highly refined sense of delicacy and honour that prevented him from being a good teller of tales, for he steadfastly refused to name the source of the gossip, the content of it or to identify the parties involved.

'Of course, some people will say that artists are like that—all passion and no common sense,' Esteban framed tight-mouthed with disapproval. 'But it is your duty to put an end to such activities and protect the family name. I am very sorry that I have had to bring this scandalous matter to your attention.'

Right up until the old man mentioned the word 'artist' and linked it with that other revealing word 'passion', Leandro had been inclined to take a humorous view of what Esteban might regard as a scandalous matter—too short a skirt? A little flirtation? A woman seen unchaperoned in male company after seven o'clock at night? But when it came to his wife's reputation, Leandro's sense of humour died. He was no more liberated than his seventeenth-century forebears who had locked up their wives and fought duels to the death over them. The only artist in his family, as far as he was concerned, was Molly.

'Fernando Santos?' he breathed between compressed lips as he shot to his feet.

Startled by that brusqueness with which that word erupted from the head of the family, Esteban nodded in grave and grudging confirmation.

To fill her time that evening, Molly was tidying up her studio. When a car drew up outside she looked out in surprise at the sight of Leandro springing out of the vehicle. He was a sleek, dark and gorgeous image in his well-cut business suit and she ate him up shamelessly with her eyes. Familiarity did not breed contempt in her experience. She might share a bed with him every night, but she remained awesomely aware of his magnificence.

Her ready smile glowed into being. 'I thought you were never going to come down and see this place,' she confided helplessly.

The faintest rise of dark colour scored the slashing cheekbones that gave Leandro's handsome face such strong lines. He glanced across the yard at the building housing the estate office and marvelled that it had not previously occurred to him that his wife was likely to become friendly with a man she was working virtually next door to several days a week.

'You've managed an impressive transformation in here,' Leandro conceded, quietly noting the scrupulous organisation and order that distinguished the studio. Molly might rush at the business of life like a tiny, intense and energetic tornado, but she did not wreak havoc on her surroundings.

'I couldn't have done it without Fernando's help. He's been invaluable. He introduced me to one of his friends who's a painter. He was able to advise me on where to buy the kiln and my supplies,' she told him.

His lean, powerful face taut and his sense of guilt

growing, for he had offered her no support, Leandro picked up a bowl with a smooth, swirling mother-of-pearl finish and examined it. 'This is very attractive, *mi cielo*. I should have done more to help and I'm relieved that Santos has made himself useful. Do you see much of him?'

Sensing his edgy mood, Molly was becoming tense. 'I see him most days—I mean, his office is only across the yard.'

Luxuriant black lashes low over his stunning dark golden eyes, Leandro held her questioning appraisal levelly. 'You need to be more careful in your dealings with him—'

'What the heck is that supposed to mean?' Molly launched at him in immediate angry interruption. 'What are you trying to imply?'

Her husband looked grim. 'I'm not implying anything. I trust you. I don't think you're foolish enough to get involved with another man, but I do think you're likely to be careless of appearances. In a rural area like this where people have old-fashioned ideas about the sexes that can cause problems.'

'I haven't done anything that anyone could take amiss!' Molly exclaimed.

'I'm afraid that you must have done because one of my relatives came to tell me about it today—'

Molly took a furious step forward. 'To talk about me? And tell you exactly *what*?'

'No specifics, just a lot of suggestive mumbling and raised brows and dark hints,' Leandro volunteered in a wry tone, reaching out for her small slender hands and enclosing them deftly in his. 'I would not discuss you with anyone. I'm just warning you to watch your step for your own sake. This isn't like London. You are a person of importance here and your every move will be noted. Our neighbours and employees do talk about us and I don't want my wife to become the focus of damaging gossip.'

'I haven't done anything that anyone could talk about—unless it was your mother. I imagine Doña Maria could come up with a pretty good story to drop me in it if she wanted to!' Molly condemned bitterly, yanking her hands free of his in a pointed gesture of condemnation.

His surprise at that response patent, Leandro frowned down at her. 'This has nothing to do with my mother—'

'You're accusing me of getting too friendly with Fernando and it's absolutely not true.'

'I've nothing more to say on this issue and I'm not going to be drawn into an argument about it.' Leandro surveyed her with forbidding cool. 'I didn't intend to upset you.'

'Of course, I'm upset. You approach me with no names, no facts and tell me to watch my every move like I'm some silly airhead of a schoolgirl likely to cause you embarrassment! Well, I may not be from a fancy aristocratic background like yours, but I do know how to behave,' she proclaimed fiercely.

'Is Santos making a nuisance of himself?' Leandro shot at her suddenly. 'Is that the problem?'

'No, *you're* the problem, Leandro!' Molly was trembling with furious resentment. It was humiliating that he should feel the need to warn her about her conduct with an employee. She shook her keys noisily and waited at the exit until he had walked past her. She then locked up the studio and stalked back towards her own vehicle.

'Leave it here. I'll take you back. I don't want you to drive in a temper,' Leandro breathed in a raw undertone, angry that she had reacted so badly to what he viewed as a mild and reasonable admonition. He was already wondering if there was more substance to the gossip than the narrow-minded rumours without foundation that he had assumed.

'I'll do whatever the hell I like!' Molly raked at him, wondering why he was so possessive of her. Evidently he didn't appreciate just how powerful a hold he had on her.

'No. You won't, *querida*,' Leandro asserted as he bent and lifted her off her startled feet to stash her bodily into the passenger seat of his car.

Molly was so taken aback by that very physical intervention that they were halfway back to the castle before she mastered her fizzing rage with him to the point where she could speak. By then she had also remembered Aloise's accident and the row that had evidently preceded that tragedy. Her tummy lurched as she understood why he had been so determined not to let her get behind the wheel in such a mood. He wouldn't talk about his precious Aloise but Molly felt positively haunted by her predecessor. She knew so many facts about Leandro's first wife but virtually nothing of a personal nature. All she had was the gorgeous blonde in the portrait in the dining room to go on for an image and the scarcely heartening knowledge that Aloise had been a successful barrister, renowned for her charity work and her talents as a hostess—an impossible act to follow as far as Molly was concerned.

'There are times when you make me so angry I could go into orbit without an engine. I can't stand being bossed around,' Molly admitted shakily. 'And I sincerely hate you when you talk down to me like I'm stupid!'

'I don't do that. You're a very passionate personality—'

'And I'm proud of it,' Molly muttered without apology.

'I'm getting used to it,' Leandro confessed, studying her delicate profile with an instinctive sense of fascination. He could feel the powerful emotion she was struggling to contain. It was that same vital life force matched with sensuality that powered their astonishingly good sex life. He rationed the time he spent with her, though. It was better that way, he told himself grimly. Everything in moderation, nothing to excess. It was the rational line to follow. He remembered how he had felt when he saw Santos responding to her sex appeal. He hadn't liked his reaction. As long as he stayed in control he need never feel that way again.

Before she went to bed, Molly logged on and checked her email box and then scolded herself for expecting a reply from Ophelia so quickly. Most probably an employee would see her email first and pass it on and it might well be some time before her sister even laid eyes on it. Maybe she had made a mistake getting in touch, she thought anxiously. Fear of rejection had kept her from travelling the road to a reunion for years, but the need to reach out to Ophelia had overwhelmed her at a vulnerable moment. All her optimistic dreams about what she might make of her marriage were slowly crumbling into dust around her.

In the spacious bedroom of her town apartment the following evening, Julieta put down her mobile phone and turned stricken eyes on to Molly, who was outlining her mouth with pillar-box-red lipstick and trying not to yawn because it was already hours after her usual bedtime. 'That was my mother…'

'I thought it might be.' Molly sighed sympathetically. 'Before I managed to get in the car to come here she told me that I was dressed like a slut and that no decent woman would go out to a nightclub without her husband.'

The leggy brunette by her side slowly shook her head in disbelief. 'I've never heard Mama in such a rage.'

'Blame me. I didn't pay any heed to her.'

'But she has no right to speak to you like that. Leandro would never stand for it. Why don't you tell him how she treats you?'

Molly shrugged. 'I don't want to get in a row with someone who's always going to be in our lives. I hoped she'd get fed up and move out.'

'It was selfish of me to invite you tonight. I don't want to cause trouble between you and Leandro. I had no idea that there were rumours that *you* were getting too friendly with Fernando!'

Molly raised a brow as she realised that her mother-in-law must already have got a hold of that tasty titbit. 'It's only silly tittle-tattle—'

'Or someone who's seen *me* at Fernando's house or in his car and made the mistake of assuming that it was you!' Julieta was unable to hide her horror at the idea that her secret relationship might be on the brink of exposure. 'Fernando is looking for another job, but he won't get one if he can't get a good reference from my brother.'

Molly tried to conceal her relief at the prospect of Fernando moving on to employment elsewhere. Angry as she was with Leandro, she felt guilty for keeping quiet about Julieta's affair and would be glad when the liaison was no longer being conducted on her doorstep. The evening before, Leandro had worked late in his study and had slept in his own room. Molly had had to fight off a powerful urge to go and join him there. Sex made her feel important and close to him, but those comforting feelings invariably evaporated in the harsh light of day. Yet, how could he be so possessive of her and not feel something for her? Were his strictures about Fernando just the male territorial instinct operating and nothing deeper?

Her mobile phone rang while she was at a fashionable tapas bar with Julieta and her friends. It was Leandro. 'Why didn't you tell me you were going out?'

'I didn't think you'd notice I was missing,' Molly heard herself reply while she smoothed down the skirt of her little black dress, which did a marvellous job of skimming her pregnant tummy.

'If you tell me where you are, I'll come and join you.'

Molly was aware that Fernando would be showing up at some stage of the evening and she knew she couldn't possibly let Leandro meet up with his sister's friends. 'No, thanks.'

'You're my wife,' Leandro growled.

'I know. Sometimes—like now—the wedding ring feels like a choke chain,' Molly told him in an undertone of helpless complaint. 'I had a lot more fun when I was single. Look, I'll see you tomorrow.'

'Tomorrow? Where are you spending the night?' Leandro raked down the line, all pretence of cool suddenly ditched.

Molly smiled wickedly, enjoying the sensation of

having surprised him. 'With your sister, of course. Please don't spoil her birthday.'

But mysteriously her bubble of enjoyment began to ebb at that point. Perhaps it was the challenge of being the only sober person in the party. Perhaps it was because, although she adored being out in company, it was already well after midnight and she was getting sleepier by the minute. Their destination was an exclusive hip club popular with the celebrity set and Fernando met up with them before they went in. A camera flash alerted Molly to the presence of the paparazzi and she was relieved to escape into the luxurious interior and sit down to watch the extravagant and entertaining floor-show.

Time began to telescope after that. She marvelled at the irony that she sat in the *castillo* most days and nights missing Leandro and that now when she'd finally got out, she was still missing him. She watched Fernando Santos conduct a very sly flirtation with one of Julieta's friends and decided that she didn't like him at all. Julieta was obviously in love, but Molly suspected that Fernando might only be with his employer's sister because she was an heiress. The music and the chatter coalesced into a droning barrage of sound and Molly's drowsiness began to gain ground on her. She fought her exhaustion because she could see that Julieta was having a great time and she was determined not to be a party-pooper. She must have dozed off at some stage, because when she stirred again she found herself outside in the night air and she only fully woke up inside the car. There were loud voices all around her and when she opened her eyes she was almost blinded by camera flashes.

'What happened...where are we going?' Molly

pulled herself up into a sitting position and addressed Julieta, who was wrapped round Fernando like a vine.

'Home. Go back to sleep,' Julieta advised, not unkindly.

Woolly-minded and with a body that felt heavy and clumsy, Molly stripped where she stood in Julieta's guest room and slept almost the same minute that her head hit the pillow. The next morning, the buzz of her mobile phone startled her and she fumbled in her bag and dug it out. Whoops, she thought in consternation even before she answered it, because there were ten missed calls listed on it. 'Molly?' a female voice exclaimed. 'Is that Molly?'

'Yes, who is this?' But Molly's heart was thumping with excitement because, although she couldn't quite believe it, she was convinced she already knew who that voice belonged to.

'Ophelia...don't you remember my voice?' her sister cried, audibly anxious. 'I wish you weren't in Spain. I want to see you right now, put my arms round you and hug you!'

And Molly burst into floods of tears and that was that. She had found her sister. Within the space of a minute the two women were catching up and soon Molly, who had never been a fan of polite pretences, found herself admitting that Leandro had only married her because she had fallen pregnant.

'You don't sound very happy,' Ophelia remarked worriedly.

'I'm not,' Molly said ruefully, but didn't add that, despite this fact, she still could not imagine living without a regular fix of her workaholic husband, because that sounded very wet and wimpy.

She was stunned when Ophelia told her that they had

an older half-brother of Russian extraction called
Nikolai Arlov. It was wonderful for her to learn that both
her siblings had been trying really hard to trace her for
several years. Ophelia was eager to satisfy Molly's curiosity about Nikolai, her children and her husband,
Lysander Metaxis. Her thoughts buzzing at the dizzy
awareness that she did have a family of her own, after
all, Molly was able to laugh out loud with pleasure
when she discovered that Haddock the parrot was still
alive.

Wrapped in a colourful silk wrap, Julieta put her
head round the door to tell Molly that the limo had
arrived to take her home and to ask her if she wanted
any breakfast before she left. Molly shook her head
and asked her sister if she could call her back later.
Awash with wondering thoughts about seeing Ophelia
again and getting to know her brother and both their
families, she dressed in the combat trousers and T-shirt
she had packed. By then she had also discovered that
most of the missed calls on her phone were from
Leandro. Guilt engulfed her and she felt remarkably like
a misbehaving teenager who had broken her curfew, and
who now had to go home to face the music.

She was dismayed to find a clutch of paparazzi
outside the apartment block, apparently awaiting her appearance. Questions were shouted at her in Spanish and
she hurried into the limo, grateful for the presence of
Leandro's security men who prevented the photogra-
phers from filming her.

She entered the castle, which was unusually silent.
Basilio greeted her oozing an attitude of funereal calm
and gloom. She was surprised when Leandro strode out
of his study, for she was aware that he had a business

trip to Geneva that day. 'I assumed you would have already left.'

'I waited to show you the morning paper.' Molly followed him into his study and glanced down enquiringly at the publication lying open on his desk. Horror seized her by the throat and she went rigid when she studied the photos on the page. One depicted a bleary-eyed and tousled woman being helped across a pavement and the second the same woman lying flat and apparently unconscious on the rear seat of a limo. That woman was her and her first foolish thought was that she had never seen more unflattering pictures. Her skirt had ridden up over her thighs and her pregnant tummy rose above them like a mountain.

'How could you get in such a condition?' Leandro raked at her furiously. 'Didn't you consider the health of the child you carry?'

'I was just very tired...I swear I wasn't drinking alcohol!' Molly protested shakily. 'The photos are very misleading—'

'You mean you weren't in a nightclub until four this morning with our estate manager? And you didn't require him to practically carry you out of it again?'

Molly swallowed hard, belatedly taking in the reality that Fernando Santos was the individual urging her shambling and sleepy self towards the car. 'I was one of a large party of people which included him.'

Her husband's strong bone structure was bone-white with tension below his bronzed skin. 'He spent the night at my sister's apartment with you. He was seen leaving early this morning!'

Molly didn't quite know what to say to that without dropping Julieta straight into a mire from which there would be no clean return. How could Leandro think that she would sleep with another man? Why did he believe she could be so untrustworthy and disloyal? She was carrying his baby. Didn't he have any respect for her at all?

'I'm not having an affair with Fernando. He's really not my type—although I have to confess that, right now, when you're standing over me like a hanging judge, you're not my type either,' Molly confided tartly. 'I'm very sorry if the photos cause you embarrassment, but I wasn't in any way under the influence of either drugs or alcohol. I was simply very, very sleepy and I have nothing else to apologise for.'

Brilliant dark eyes cut into hers like abrasive diamond cutters. 'I don't believe you. I want the truth…'

'I've told you the truth.' Molly was torn between feeling hugely intimidated and hugely resentful that he could have so little faith in her that he instantly dismissed her explanation. 'I went out with Julieta to celebrate her birthday.'

'Then why wouldn't you tell me where you were so that I could join you?'

Molly shuffled her feet, knowing that there was no acceptable answer to that and wishing she didn't feel obligated to cover up for Julieta's private life. It was not a friendship she wanted to put at risk. 'I just wanted a night off from being your wife. Is that a crime?'

His classic features hardened at that facetious response. 'How long have you been seeing Santos?'

'Maybe you'd like me to be an unfaithful wife and then you would have grounds for divorcing me. Is that what this is about? You've realised that you made a mistake marrying me and you want an escape route?' Molly slung at him accusingly.

'You're talking nonsense,' Leandro drawled icily.

'No, I'm not. I want an escape route!' Molly threw at him in a rage. 'I want my life back, so why shouldn't you? You're an absentee husband and I'm lonely. I want a man who's interested me and who I can share stuff with. But you're so busy making money and putting everything else ahead of me, you don't have time for me or the baby that's coming. Why shouldn't I want more than your precious money, your title and social position? None of those things are important to me!'

'You've said enough,' Leandro intoned with ferocious bite, mentally stacking up those far-reaching accusations as a clumsy attempt to deflect him from her inexcusable behaviour. 'I still have a flight to Geneva to catch. I'll see you tomorrow.'

'You said you couldn't give me love—but what *have* you given me?' Molly whispered chokily.

Leandro ground his even white teeth together. He refused to listen to her. He didn't want her to start crying. He was so angry with her that he didn't trust himself to speak. As long as she continued to deny everything, there was nothing to discuss and no way forward. He would get the truth out of Julieta, and if Molly had betrayed his trust he would have no choice but to divorce her. But having reached that pinnacle of masculine decisiveness, Leandro discovered that that obvious solution had zero appeal for him. He pictured Molly in Santos's arms and he felt as if someone were trying to rip his guts out with a machete. The black rage tamped down inside him surged higher and the fierce struggle it took to stay in control angered him even more.

Molly couldn't believe that Leandro was still planning to fly off to Geneva just as if nothing had happened. His rock-hard self-discipline and devotion to banking business when their marriage was in crisis struck her as yet more proof of his lack of caring. Her mobile phone rang just as she reached the sanctuary of her bedroom. The instant she heard her sister's voice, her control over her tumultuous emotions dissolved. Suddenly she was in floods of tears and struggling to find the right words to answer Ophelia's concerned questions. Unfortunately there was no pleasant way to explain that Leandro was convinced that she had been carrying on an affair with one of his employees. Her sister was very shocked by that admission and then she explained that she was with their brother, Nikolai, who also wanted to speak to her. Somewhere just out of Molly's hearing at the other end of the line she could hear an urgent discussion taking place between her newly discovered siblings.

'Do you really want to stay with this bozo in Spain?' a very forceful masculine voice enquired a little while later. 'I can pick you up in a few hours and fly you back to England.'

Molly was shaken by the idea of leaving Spain within hours, but it was a remarkably tempting offer when she was in dire need of comfort and support. 'Could you...I mean, would you?'

'I'm very impatient to meet my baby sister,' Nikolai confessed bluntly.

'I'm not a baby—'

'You are on my terms,' he countered with uncompromising bluntness.

Feverish indecision assailed Molly. She desperately wanted to be with her sister and meet her brother. Leandro had devastated her to the extent that she could barely think straight. He had accused her of infidelity and paid no heed to her denials. He had shown no sign of even being prepared to listen to her perfectly reasonable complaints. Was she really planning to sit and wait for him to return from Geneva for more of the same? He didn't love her. Nothing was likely to change that. She was never going to compare to Aloise and the fact that she was expecting his baby in another few months currently seemed to be a matter of near indifference to him. Perhaps he had decided that marrying her had been a mistake. That could explain why he had made little effort to make their marriage a success.

Molly squared her slight shoulders and breathed in deep. 'I'll come back home with you.'

Nikolai promised to call her when his jet landed in Spain. Ophelia was so excited when she came back on the phone that Molly could only follow about one word in three, but her sister's enthusiasm melted the cold knot of fear and uncertainty forming inside her.

She sat down at the elegant ladies desk by the window and pulled out the fancy stationery she had never used to write Leandro a note. Tears were streaming down her tight face while she studied the blank sheet of paper in anguish. What she was feeling was forcing her to acknowledge that she cared a great deal more about Leandro than he cared about her. But she didn't want to be the sort of sad woman who settled for the crumbs from the table because she lacked the pride to believe that she deserved the whole loaf. If she was unhappy, her child would be unhappy as well. Her dream of creating a happy home and family for the three of them was exactly that: just a dream and not an achievable goal with Leandro in a leading role.

She was packing when she made a curious discovery while she was searching for a missing shoe at the back of a closet. Her fingers encountered a surprising lump below the carpet on the floor of the cupboard and she pushed it back and drew out what had lain concealed underneath. To her astonishment she realised that she was holding several packets of birth control pills. Now, who on earth would have hidden a secret stash of contraceptives there? And her imagination could only come up with one likely contender—Aloise, whose evident inability to fall pregnant might seemingly have been a deliberate choice. So the perfect wife had not been quite so perfect, after all. Molly shrugged and put the pills back where she had found them.

She left all her jewellery behind and even removed her rings to leave them lying on the dressing table. After a light lunch served in her room, she went for a nap from which she was wakened by Nikolai's call. Having dressed again, she rang for a member of staff to carry down her cases. Basilio was at the foot of the staircase, wringing his hands. She thought painfully of how much Leandro would loathe the attention that the breakdown of their marriage would create. Her baby kicked and she tensed, wondering guiltily if her child could somehow feel her emotional turmoil.

Doña Maria appeared in the doorway of the salon. The older woman looked incredibly smug, but Molly couldn't have cared less, for she could already hear the noisy approach of a helicopter flying in low. That was the exact moment that what she was doing really sank in on her, not the best time for her to realise that she had fallen in love with Leandro when she was in the midst of wondering how he had survived his cold and severe mother's upbringing. But she didn't need to wonder, did she? Leandro had developed self-reliance and rigid self-discipline at a very early age while learning to hide and suppress his emotions.

Someone rapped noisily on the front door. Basilio opened it. Molly saw a very tall and powerfully built man with dark hair striding towards the entrance while body-guards fanned out around him. In the background sat a helicopter with Arlov Industries written across the tail.

'Molly?' he queried with a wide measuring apprai-sal, and then he flung back his handsome head and laughed, impervious to Doña Maria's goggling stare at him, his men and his helicopter. 'I don't believe it— you're even smaller than Ophelia!'

He snapped his fingers and one of his bodyguards hurried forward to lift her luggage. She walked out into the sunshine and part of her screamed to stay. Her nerves were stretched tight as piano wires.

'You're not sure about doing this, are you?' her com-panion divined with disturbing ease.

'I don't think I've any other option right now.'

Nikolai Arlov paused in his stride and rested his shrewd gaze on her troubled face. 'As a husband, I should warn you that your Spanish duke won't forgive this move in a hurry.'

Molly shrugged a feisty shoulder while she thought of all the evenings that had stretched into eternity as she had spent them alone. 'I'll survive,' she replied with determination.

'So, is this an I'm-leaving-you-for-ever or I-want-you-to-sit-up-and-take-notice walkout?' Nikolai enquired lazily.

Molly registered that her big brother knew a lot about women. 'The jury's still out on that one.'

'Because he went to Geneva? But that was work,' Nikolai pointed out, as if putting business first was a perfectly understandable act.

Sudden tears burned at the backs of her eyes. Too much was happening all at once. Her chin tilting, she blinked rapidly. She had got by before Leandro and she would get by after him just as well. But she still had to learn how to *want* to do that, she acknowledged heavily. The helicopter took off and she watched the *castillo* ebbing from view and wondered just when she would see Leandro again and whether or not lawyers would be present at the occasion.

CHAPTER NINE

LEANDRO studied his bruised knuckles with little sense of satisfaction. He had visited Santos on the way to the airport and had found the estate manager in the act of loading up his car, apparently already aware that his secret was out. A hopeless opponent, Santos had mumbled apologies and ducked a fight. How could Molly have been attracted to a man with all the backbone of a worm?

Flying out to Geneva, regardless of events, had proved a mistake. His concentration had evaporated as increasingly nightmarish images of Molly in another man's bed had interrupted his usual rational thinking processes. He had cut his meetings short to fly home. Once there, he had enjoyed an exchange of opinions with his mother that had led to her fuming departure within the space of an hour. Only then had he had the privacy to walk up to Molly's abandoned bedroom.

Her exit note was a tangled tale of the new and lately rediscovered family relationships that had led to her flight in Nikolai Arlov's helicopter. Nikolai Arlov, Leandro reflected heavily. Her brother was a Russian billionaire. But the emptiness of the room had affected

Leandro much more than the revelations on paper. Her rings lay on the dressing table in rejection of their marriage. He could picture her yanking them off, green eyes blazing with anger and defiance. He could still see the indent of her tiny body on the bedspread where she had lain down. The imagery paralysed him and his fists clenched in a bitter battle with the churning emotions he had refused to acknowledge throughout the day.

He was envisaging a world without Molly and it would be a world shorn of colour or warmth. Every morning she got up to have breakfast with him and chattered tirelessly through the meal he had once enjoyed in the strictest silence with his newspapers. Now he would have the peace back and the *castillo* would echo around him again. He would no longer have her to come home to, a beacon at the end of a long working day spent in meetings or travelling. But that was as it should be, wasn't it? What odds when she had been unfaithful and only a divorce could settle their differences? But he was not capable of such cool logic. He could not get beyond one basic fact: her bed was empty and she was gone.

Someone knocked on the door and he swung round to refuse that invasion of his privacy. But it was Julieta, his younger sister, who stood flushed and tear-stained in the doorway.

'I don't want to talk to anyone right now,' Leandro breathed not quite steadily.

'Even if I'm here to tell you that I'm the one who was having the affair with Fernando?' Julieta sobbed.

There were three women in the swimming pool.

Molly lay back on her floating couch and sipped at her strawberry smoothie while twitching her toes to the beat of the dance track playing in the unashamedly luxurious pool house at Nikolai's London home.

'You're looking better,' Abbey, her brother's red-headed, beautiful and equally pregnant wife, pronounced with approval as she awkwardly got down to towel dry her son. Danilo was a wriggling, laughing toddler with a good deal of his father's forceful personality.

'You were as pale as a waif when you arrived,' Ophelia opined. 'Now you're eating proper meals and much more relaxed.'

Molly smiled, more than satisfied with the family circle she had found and got to know over the past week. She had spent the first few days with Ophelia and Lysander at Madrigal Court, where she had also got to know her niece and nephews, the youngest of whom was only four months old. Nikolai had insisted that DNA testing should be carried out so that no one could ever question her identity, and the tests had also revealed a connection that Molly had never suspected before.

Her father, it seemed, had definitely been the Greek tycoon, Aristide Metaxis, the man who had not only jilted her unfortunate mother at the altar, but who had also become Cathy's long-term lover in later years. Molly did, in fact, have a vague memory of a male visitor, who had often given her sweets. It had fascinated her that Aristide's adoptive son, Lysander, who was Ophelia's husband, should also be her adoptive half-brother. What was more, that particular relationship would have lasting effects on her life, for, apparently, Aristide had discreetly left money in trust for an unnamed child and his lawyers were convinced that

that child was Molly and that he had been well aware at the time of his death that he had a daughter.

Abbey answered the house phone by her side and then gave Molly a speculative smile. 'Your husband is here to see you.'

Molly began paddling like mad for the side of the pool with Ophelia, an unflappable blonde, following suit at a leisurely crawl. She climbed out and caught the towel that Abbey tossed to her, wrapping it round her to warm suddenly chilled skin. A whole week had elapsed since she'd left Spain. Leandro had taken his time to come looking for her. Cramming her bare feet into flip-flops, she headed into the lift to go upstairs.

Her heart was thundering in her eardrums as she padded into the opulent drawing room and she was as out of breath as though she had been running. Leandro was a very tall, still figure by the front windows. He swung round, brilliant dark eyes zeroing in on her small figure. Her casual appearance startled him. With her black curls anchored on top of her head with a clip and a bright tangerine bikini top showing above the edges of the black and yellow towel she wore, Molly took him very much by surprise.

Superbly well dressed in a black pinstripe designer suit that was tailored to enhance every muscular angle of his lean, powerful body, Leandro had a pure physical impact that engulfed Molly like a wave breaking over her head that left her struggling for breath. A masculine dream of black hair, golden skin and lustrous dark heavily lashed eyes, he looked stunning to a woman whose senses had been starved of his presence. This, after all, was the guy she woke up searching for in her bed at night. Her breasts swelled and her body tingled back to life at the mere sight of him.

'Your brother refused to tell me where you were,' Leandro growled soft and low, but with all the warning threat of a tiger flexing his claws.

Molly tensed. 'Honestly? I had no idea—'

'I first made contact with him by phone when he was flying you back to London on the day you left a week ago.' Leandro volunteered that information grimly. 'He said you didn't want to speak to me.'

Molly went pink, furious that Nikolai had chosen to make such decisions on her behalf and resenting his interference in her marriage. 'He shouldn't have done that, but he was probably trying to protect me.'

'I owe you a sincere apology for my misconceptions about your relationship with Fernando Santos,' Leandro delivered gravely, his striking dark golden eyes welded to hers. 'Julieta told me the truth.'

'Oh…' Off-balanced by his immediate apology, Molly couldn't concentrate. 'I haven't spoken to her since I left. Is she all right?'

'She was very upset about what happened between us and she's broken up with Santos, after finding out that she wasn't the only woman in his life. I think that in the circumstances you should have told me the truth.'

Molly drew herself up to her full insignificant height and breathed in deep. 'You wouldn't have believed me! From the first moment you saw Fernando talking to me, you were suspicious of us—'

'*Dios mio*, I was jealous,' Leandro admitted between gritted teeth. 'I immediately saw his eagerness to impress you, his admiration for you.'

'For me, and I don't know how many other women.

Fernando is a self-satisfied flirt,' Molly cut in, ever so slightly mollified by that unexpected confession of jealousy. 'I thought you didn't get jealous.'

His incredible cheekbones tensed. 'I believed that was the truth when I said it to you. I didn't recognise what a hold jealousy had got on my mind, so that I misinterpreted everything that happened to fit my deepest…er…fears.' His accented drawl dropped in level as he fitted in that last revealing word, low and quick. 'Of course you were correct when you said that I should have trusted you. But you're a very beautiful, sensual young woman and why should other men not be knocked out by you as I was?'

Her towel was slipping, revealing an eye-catching depth of cleavage. Conscious of his gaze dropping to the cups struggling to restrain her bountiful breasts, Molly reddened and hoisted her towel. Even so, her treacherous body was already reacting to that interest with a hot pulse low in her pelvis.

'How could you just walk out on our marriage?' Leandro demanded.

'Easily. I was the only person making an effort in our relationship. You were never there and you made me live with your mother, who absolutely hated me!'

'I wasn't aware how deep her dislike of you was until she voiced certain opinions to me after you had gone. She's returned to her home in Seville and is now aware that she is not welcome at the *castillo* unless she can treat you with the respect that is your right as my wife. Why did I have to wait for my mother to lose her temper to find out how she was treating you? Why didn't you just tell me?'

It was a fair question, Molly acknowledged. 'I didn't

know whose side you would take and I didn't want to put you in that position. I honestly did believe that sooner or later Doña Maria would get tired of needling me and just accept me.'

'But you deserved better than that in your own home. Naturally I would have taken your side. I have no illusions about what my mother can be like—'

'I think she was behind the financial offer that was made to me before I married you,' Molly said abruptly.

'What financial offer?'

Molly gave him the details. He was staggered, genuinely staggered, when she shared the content of that meeting. He asked her to name the legal firm concerned and a flash of recognition lit his hard gaze. 'That firm did work for the estate at one time. It is very likely that my mother was behind that offer. I had no idea that she would go to such extremes or even that she would dare to interfere in my life to that extent—'

'She doesn't think I'm good enough for you.'

His anger was palpable and his strong jaw line clenched. '*Dios mio*, you turned down two million pounds to marry me?'

'Yeah…I'd have been wiser grabbing the cash and running for the hills, wouldn't I?' she quipped in a wry allusion to the current state of their relationship.

Leandro took a sudden step forward, his spectacular dark golden gaze narrowed and intent. 'I am very grateful that you didn't and that you went through with our marriage. I only wish I had done more with the opportunity.'

'No, I don't think you do,' Molly contradicted with a rueful grimace. 'You didn't want any more than a shallow show of a marriage for the baby's sake, but, unfortunately, I'm not as detached as you are. I couldn't live like that for the rest of my days.'

'Why didn't you speak to me sooner about how you felt?' Leandro prompted grimly. 'Didn't it occur to you that the day I believed you had spent the night with a lover was not the right moment to tackle me about my deficiencies as a husband?'

'No. As I hadn't been with a lover, that angle didn't occur to me,' Molly conceded.

'I had spent the whole night worrying about you. Again, it's all my own fault,' he framed in a harsh undertone. 'Your brother, Nikolai, left me in no doubt of that. Had you had bodyguards the paparazzi would never have got near you and I would have known where you were that night.'

'I don't need bodyguards. Nikolai is extremely security conscious.'

Leandro reached for her hands, which she was unconsciously wringing, and closed them firmly into his. Determined dark golden eyes locked with her anxious gaze. 'I am not detached from you, nor do I wish to be. I want you back, *mi corazón*. I would have told you that a week ago, had your brother been willing to tell me where you were.'

Molly tensed, hope and doubt warring inside her in a death-defying tussle of seething conflict. 'I'm sure you mean well, but marriage for me has to be about more than you doing the right thing for the woman carrying your child. I would never try to shut you out of our baby's life.'

His grip on her hands was almost painfully tight. 'How do I convince you that it will be different? This is not about doing the right thing. I'm asking you to give me the chance to *prove* how much I value your presence in my life.'

Tears were burning her eyes. This was the guy she loved, the guy she missed every hour of the day, and once again he was offering her what she craved, only this time around she was less naive. 'But the point is that you didn't value me when I was there. You didn't even come home for dinner at night. You didn't phone me. You didn't look for me or show the smallest sign that you missed me when you were away from me.'

Leandro was pale as death beneath his bronzed complexion and his handsome bone structure was rigid with ferocious tension. 'I have never found it easy to show my feelings. I would not allow myself to need you too much. I saw that as a weakness and I do not like to be in anything other than full control.'

'Whereas I let everything show, and say and do what I feel like. We're a very bad match, Leandro. I was lonely and unhappy with you and I don't want to go back to that,' she confided jerkily, fighting off temptation with all her strength because she refused to end up back where she had started. 'Now that the break has been made, it should get easier for us both.'

'I don't like my life without you in it!' Leandro launched at her rawly in the roughest tone she had ever heard from him.

'I think you should go,' Molly pronounced tightly.

'I can't walk away from you and my child!' he bit out in a driven undertone.

'You have to, if that's what she wants,' another male voice interposed from the doorway.

Molly turned her head to see her adoptive half-brothers poised just inside the room, neither of them looking particularly welcoming. 'Nikolai—stay out of this, *please*!'

Fierce aggression powered through Leandro's powerful frame when he recognised the level of family opposition in the two men's faces. 'Are you with Nikolai on this, Lysander?' he asked grimly.

'No, I don't believe in interfering in other people's marriages,' the tall handsome Greek breathed with measured calm. 'But if you cause my sister any more grief, I'll rip you apart!'

The Russian tycoon studied Leandro with cold hostility. 'Molly has us now. She doesn't need anyone else.'

'Let's allow Molly to make that decision,' Leandro countered, striding to the door and looking back at Molly to say, 'You know where I'm staying.'

Molly swallowed the lump in her throat and nodded. Every fibre of her being urged her to chase after him and stop him from leaving her. It took every ounce of her self-discipline to let him go without a murmur. She told herself that she had made the wisest decision. She didn't want to be the second-best wife of a man who didn't love her. She didn't want to spend her life saving face by hiding her love for him. She wanted to be brave and independent: she had to learn how to get by without him.

Nikolai patted her taut shoulder as the front door closed on Leandro's departure. 'You made the right decision.'

'Only if it's what Molly really wants,' Lysander interposed seriously, shooting her pale face an unconvinced appraisal.

'Molly and I both grew up without a silver spoon in our mouths.' Nikolai intoned that reminder flatly. 'What do you think she has in common with a duke who went to a British public school?'

'He's really not a snob,' Molly mumbled helplessly in Leandro's favour.

'They will soon have a child in common.' Lysander dealt his brother-in-law an impatient glance. 'And that child is a good enough reason for Molly to take her time over deciding whether or not she wants a divorce.'

Divorce! That very word struck horror into Molly's bones. Divorce would be so final. She would never see Leandro again unless he came to visit their child and she did not think she could bear the prospect of that. That conviction grew on her while she played with her brothers' children that evening. Surely when she loved Leandro so much it made sense to give their marriage one more chance? Soon after reaching that conclusion, she told Abbey that she was going over to Leandro's apartment to see him.

One of Nikolai's security team tagged her all the way to the door and it was a relief to step inside. Leandro focused on her with frowning force, her appearance clearly coming as a surprise to him. The smell of whiskey clinging to him took her by surprise for Leandro rarely drank. In addition, he was not his usual perfectly groomed self. His tie was missing, his jacket crumpled and he badly needed a shave.

'Molly?' he queried, as if he couldn't quite accept the evidence of his own eyes.

Molly leant back against the door and walked past him into the airy lounge where a half-empty whisky bottle and a single glass sat beside an untouched meal. 'I have a proposition to put to you,' she stated.

Leandro gave her an enquiring look, which would have been more impressive had his eyes been in focus and had he contrived to walk in a straight line. In actuality he managed neither, for her abstemious husband was anything but sober. 'Go ahead.'

'A make-or-break holiday of at least three weeks for just the two of us, to see if we can make something of this marriage,' Molly murmured, wondering why he was drinking alone and worrying about it.

'I can do that!' Leandro declared instantly.

'Leandro…in Spain you couldn't do one night at home with me, so don't underestimate what you'd be signing up for,' she sighed.

His lean, strong features set into purposeful strong lines. 'I'll try anything that means I don't lose you and the baby, *mi preciosa*.'

Her eyes shone with tears, for she realised that he had done some serious thinking and was finally recognising what the breakdown of their marriage would ultimately cost him. Naturally he didn't want to lose the chance to bring up the child he had married her to support. 'And no more secrets. I know you're not the sort of guy who's in touch with his feelings, but you still have them…don't you?'

Leandro studied her, poised there in a bright red raincoat with her dark curly head tilted to one side like a little inquisitive bird, and snatched in a ragged breath. '*Sí.*'

'So that's the deal: long holiday, no secrets, major effort on all fronts from you,' Molly proffered anxiously.

'Do you want to go now?' Leandro enquired hopefully.

'No, I think you should sleep off the whisky first,' Molly said wryly. 'What about tomorrow afternoon? Could you hire a villa somewhere?'

'It's done. It will be the holiday of a lifetime,' Leandro swore…

CHAPTER TEN

THE Casa Limone sat in a breathtaking Tuscan land-scape of woods and hills. A Renaissance jewel with ancient walls and a tower, the former farmhouse enjoyed a contrastingly cool and contemporary interior. Surrounded by olive groves, vines and rolling fields speckled with glorious wild flowers, the house lay at the foot of a long lane in a sunlit glade of perfect peace and seclusion.

Molly was surprised when Leandro admitted that it was only one of the houses he had bought as an investment over the years and put in the charge of a rental agency. He had never mentioned his extensive property portfolio to her before. A tense expression suddenly gripped her small face as she stepped out of the four-wheel drive they had picked up at the airport. 'Did you ever bring *her* here? Aloise, I mean?' she clarified, hating herself for asking, but, all the same, desperately needing to know.

'No.' As if realising that that one defensive word was insufficient, Leandro added, 'She preferred the city.'

'Oh...' Registering that she had got a whole sentence

dug out of him on that controversial issue, Molly didn't waste time about going in for the kill. 'Was it really a perfect marriage?'

The silence seemed to thunder in her sensitive ears.

'No,' Leandro breathed curtly. 'We were both miserable.'

And with that stunning response he might as well have gagged Molly. She was so shocked that she could think of nothing else to say. Her gaze locked to his tight profile and the moment was lost as he lifted their cases to take them indoors. In a handful of words, he had blown away her conviction that their relationship came a poor second to his first marital excursion. Suddenly she was on unfamiliar ground and wondering how to be subtle and tactful, rather than shamelessly eager to hear every wretched detail that had contributed to that mutual misery.

Yet how could she have been so blind to the obvious? Was it surprising that the guy who didn't like weddings had good reason for his prejudice? People were more likely to talk about happy memories, but Leandro never voluntarily mentioned Aloise's name and only now was she realising what had lain hidden behind that silence.

'What were Nikolai's last words to you today?' Leandro asked, startling her out of her reverie.

'Abbey wished us well!' Molly ducked the issue to tell him brightly. 'Nikolai just hasn't had the chance to get to know you yet and you met under the wrong circumstances.'

'But what did he say?' Leandro persisted.

'That if I can't be myself with you, it'll never work,' she divulged in an apprehensive rush.

A grim smile shadowed his wide sensual mouth. 'He's shrewd.'

'But so are you.' And gorgeous and clever and the man I love, Molly added inside her head.

'I thought I was until you took off your wedding ring,' Leandro confided in a dark, deep, abrasive drawl that shimmied down her spine like a burst of electrical energy on a still day.

Molly focused on his lean darkly handsome features, her heart buzzing like a battery-driven toy inside her chest. She had feared that she might never be so close to him again. The future had become a terrifying destination that she was afraid to face. She had lost faith in her own judgement, had questioned what she had done and the impossibility of undoing it. The pain of leaving him, of being without him, had coloured everything she thought and experienced. Just at that instant, the pure relief of being with him again made her knees turn weak.

Leandro's attention dropped to the lush pink contours of her mouth. 'Do you want your rings back?'

Molly froze, evasive eyes reflecting her insecurity. 'Let's see how things go.'

Brilliant dark eyes challenged her. 'Am I on trial?'

Molly moved her hands in a soothing motion and tried to explain what she felt. 'I suppose we both are. I don't want us to break up after our child's got used to us being together, so if we can't work things out it would be better if we separated before the birth.'

Leandro was spooked by her earnest tone, the clear fact that she had considered such matters in depth. He leant forward, splaying his hands to the painted wall on either side of her, imprisoning her there. Dark golden eyes fired down into hers. 'I will fight long and hard to keep you—'

'But it's not a failure to lose this battle,' Molly whispered urgently. 'It would just mean that we're not suited but that we did our best. I don't want you to stay with me only because of the baby.'

A rather ragged laugh escaped Leandro. 'That's not why I'm here. I'm here because I want *you*, *tesora mia*...' a lean brown forefinger shifted to probe the peachy softness of her full lips, lingering when they parted '...and I've spent a week living with the idea that I might never be able to be with you again...'

'Me too,' Molly confided, shaken that on one score at least they could think the exact same thoughts.

'And now that's all I can think about,' he confessed in a driven undertone. 'But that's not what you want from me at this moment.'

'No?'

Black lashes semi-screened his gaze. 'Of course, it isn't,' he told her with assurance. 'You want to talk and sit down to a romantic meal and then maybe go for a walk.'

She could tell this programme of civilised restraint had as much appeal for him at that instant as having his teeth pulled without an anaesthetic and she almost laughed out loud. Evidently he had thought a great deal about what she might expect from him and if he was getting it wrong, it was only because he had yet to grasp what she most wanted from him.

'Maybe tomorrow we could do that. Right now I want your time and your attention—which is all I ever wanted. There isn't some magical success-guaranteed blueprint of an itinerary to follow, even though I can see you wish there was.' She lifted her hands and began to unbutton his shirt. 'Whatever both of us want is perfect. We only have ourselves to please.'

He laced a possessive hand into her tumbling mane of curls, his other hand closing to her hip to tilt her against him. His mouth came down on hers with a raw, hot hunger that made no attempt to deny its urgency. The erotic plunge of his tongue provoked a surge of moisture between her thighs and she shivered convulsively in spite of the heat. She broke the kiss to finish unbuttoning the shirt and finally spread her hands across his bronzed hair-roughened torso, letting her fingers stroke and explore down to the intriguing silky furrow that disappeared below his belt while remaining awesomely aware of the revealing bulge beneath his chinos. Trembling, mortified by her own eagerness, she drew back from him, closed one hand over his and began to move towards the stairs.

'You want me too,' Leandro said thickly, his satisfaction unhidden.

'Shut up, or you'll get ravished on the stairs,' Molly warned him.

In response to that threat, Leandro pulled her slight, swollen body to him and kissed her with a passion that blew her away. He removed her dress in a shaded room where muslin panels swished across the chestnut-wood floor in the faint cooling breeze coming in through the open windows. Birds were singing in the woods behind the house. A swelling sense of happiness blossomed inside her, as if only now was she finally able to believe that she was back with Leandro.

She slid onto cool linen sheets and felt him hard, hot and rampant against her thigh and gloried in the differences between them. He stroked the full, firm globes of her breasts, lingering with tender care on the swollen pink buds of her nipples. She was all restive energy and craving, controlled by the pulsing ache in her pelvis. Everything was happening just a moment later than she needed it to happen.

'Leandro, please…' she framed, her voice tight with stress and longing.

'Trust me,' he breathed huskily. 'It'll be better this way.'

Her hips shifted up to him. She was way past caring about the exact shades of satisfaction; she was more than willing to settle for the most basic kind of all. Even before he touched the most receptive spot on her entire body she was burning up, liquid with desire and unbearably sensitive. The sound of her moans made him crush her reddened lips below his again. Her impatience tormented her, her need more fundamental than any she had ever known before.

Leandro turned her gently on her side, eased her back against him and entered her with a sweet, piercing depth that made her cry out in surprise and pleasure. And as he had promised it only got better. His slow, insistent rhythm was indescribably sensual and extremely controlled. Her excitement climbed to torturous heights as waves of pleasure began to pulse through her. She reached a shattering climax and tears wet her eyes at the wonderful intensity of her release. But nothing could have been more precious to her than the moment when Leandro vented an ecstatic groan and spilled inside her. He closed his arms tightly round her and pressed his mouth to her shoulder, muttering incomprehensible words of Spanish.

Right then at that pinnacle of happiness she recognised how fierce and elemental their hunger to make love again had been. They had needed to rediscover and share that intimacy after their separation, brief though it had been.

His fingers flexed against the swell of her stomach as the baby kicked and he lifted his tousled dark head. 'Is that our child moving?'

Molly confirmed that it was. He kept his hand in place before finally turning her round to face him and holding her close. 'I've signed you up with a local gynaecologist for the duration of our stay.'

'That wasn't necessary.' But Molly was secretly impressed that he had thought to take that precaution.

'I felt that it was, *tesora mia*,' Leandro intoned. 'Just in case we need to consult a doctor while you're here. I'm coming with you the next time you have a scan.'

'Only if you want to.'

His ebony brows pleated. 'I always wanted to, but I thought you might find my presence an intrusion at such appointments. You never showed any sign of wanting me to accompany you.'

It dawned on her that he had felt excluded and doubtful in a situation that was new and unfamiliar to him. She shifted closer and touched her mouth softly to his. 'I assumed you'd know that I wanted you there for support, but I didn't say anything about it because I didn't want you to feel obligated to go. I knew how busy you were.'

'A man who is too busy for his family doesn't deserve one, *querida*. My father died when I was five and I barely remember him. I was in boarding school a year later.'

Molly frowned. 'That's much too young to be sent away from home.'

'I think so, too. In fact, I don't believe I would send my child away to board. There is no harm in breaking with tradition for a new generation.'

The following morning they visited a charming gynaecologist, whose name had been recommended to Leandro. Molly had a scan there and then at the private clinic and was amused and touched by Leandro's fascination with their unborn son and the keen questions he asked. It occurred to her that her fear of being snubbed had ensured that she made no attempt to share any aspect of her pregnancy with him. She was warmed by the concern he couldn't hide when the doctor advised that their child be delivered by Caesarean section because the baby was big and she was small.

'Are you sure babies like bright colours that much?' Leandro studied the vibrant cot quilt and blinked quite deliberately.

'According to all the research…yes,' Molly declared.

'Colour is not my thing, *mi corazón*,' Leandro admitted evenly as they walked back towards the car in the enveloping warmth of late afternoon. He ushered her into a seat in the shade at a pavement café. 'Sit down. You're tired.'

Molly gave him a sleepy smile. If truth be known, she was tired of being pregnant, weary of hauling a larger, heavier body everywhere she went and sick of being clumsy and prone to tripping over her own feet. Yet a glorious sense of contentment washed over her as Leandro hailed the waiter and in fluent Italian ordered her favourite ice cream, a glass of wine for him and a long cold drink for her. They had sat on that particular terrace enjoying the view of the vineyards in the valley below many times, for the picturesque little hill town lay within a short drive of the house.

Their four-week sojourn in Tuscany had taught Molly that she could always relax when Leandro was around. He was great at looking after her and amazingly good at foreseeing her every need. She noticed a couple of women watching him with appreciation from a nearby table. They fancied the socks off him just as she did. She was always worrying that she betrayed her love when she looked at him. She worked hard at keeping things light and cool. He had been so upfront right from the start when he had admitted that he couldn't give her love. She was determined not to make him uncomfortable and risk destroying what they did have, purely because she couldn't settle for what she had got.

And she *had* settled for what she had with him; it was official. Last night she had put her rings back on and she had noticed that every so often he rested his attention on her hand, as if he liked to see them there on her finger.

Over the past month she had gradually let go of all her fears and allowed herself to be content. The shadow of Aloise had evaporated and Molly no longer tormented herself with futile comparisons. Even if Aloise had been the love of Leandro's life, their marriage had not worked out and Molly could no longer feel unequal or envious. She was still curious, still planning on telling Leandro about the contraceptive pills she had found, but she was too happy to want to risk spoiling the ambience they had achieved.

They had had a wonderful honeymoon six months after their wedding. She had strolled along the city ramparts at Lucca, wandered through the medieval streets of Florence and Siena, occasionally pausing to explore ancient buildings and admire spectacular art at a leisurely pace. A hundred special memories had ensured she would never forget their time at Casa Limone. The scent of new-mown grass would forever remind her of making love in the lemon orchard beside the house and lying drowsing in the languorous aftermath in Leandro's arms until it was almost dinner time. In the same way the taste of glorious chocolate would always remind her of being pregnant. She lusted after that wonderful taste-bud-melting flavour almost as much and as continuously as she lusted after Leandro, who didn't know what a full night's uninterrupted sleep was. He had confessed that he felt badly misled by the book he had read that suggested that a woman's interest in sex would wane as her pregnancy advanced.

Propping her chin on the heel of her hand, Molly surveyed her vibrantly handsome husband with dreamy appreciation. He was gorgeous and she felt that wanting to touch him pretty frequently was normal because sometimes she just couldn't believe her good luck in having him and needed to satisfy herself that he really was hers in every way that mattered.

'Are you thinking about our flight back to Spain tomorrow? Your family will be staying with us this weekend,' Leandro reminded her.

Molly smiled, recognising his concern that she might be less than eager to return to the *castillo*, but that wasn't the case. On the contrary, she was looking forward to the prospect. She was confident that everything would be different this time around. After all, Doña Maria was no longer in residence and Molly's marital home would finally be her own. To give him his due, Leandro had been appalled when he had realised that Molly had been prevented from having any input into the household arrangements and his mother had lied when she had announced that that had been his idea.

'I can't wait to see Ophelia again,' she admitted.

'But the two of you are always talking on the phone,' Leandro pointed out with a shake of his dark head.

'You'll be going back to work the day after tomorrow,' Molly said ruefully, knowing that that was normal life but dreading it all the same, for she had adored having him around all the time.

Dark golden eyes level, Leandro brushed the back of her hand in a perceptive gesture. 'I won't work the hours I used to. I won't be travelling for a while either and I'll phone you at least twice a day.'

'The sun is gleaming over your halo,' Molly teased.

'It's very important to me that you be happy.'

As she was convinced that he would have taken his first marriage equally seriously, she could not help wondering what had gone so badly wrong. That evening they dined out at a little restaurant they had visited before. On the drive home, she said softly, 'Tell me about Aloise…'

'She was all things to all people. Her family idolised her. Her colleagues admired her. I regarded her as a very close friend. Our families began pushing us together when we were in our mid-twenties. I'd enjoyed my freedom up until that point and I assumed she had as well. We could have said no, but our marriage seemed to make sense. I thought we wanted the same things out of life and you know I'm not the romantic type,' Leandro told her confidently in spite of the fact that he had lit pink candles round the hot tub and scattered rose petals on the water for her.

'So you saw your marriage as a practical arrangement?'

'I thought Aloise had the same view. She wasn't any more in love than I was, but she was very feminine and, naturally, I found her attractive After the wedding, our friendship just seemed to die. I didn't know what was wrong and she insisted that there *was* nothing wrong,' he breathed in a driven undertone.

They walked into the villa. Molly put on lights. 'What happened the day of the accident?'

Leandro dealt her a cloaked look. 'What I tell you must remain private for the sake of her family. She didn't want them to find out.' The silence hummed and his hand clenched taut as he made an awkward movement with it. 'I demanded to know why she was treating me like an enemy. So, she finally told me the truth and I lost my temper with her…'

'How?' she whispered, her attention welded to his haunted expression in the lamplight.

'I accused her of deceiving me and ruining both our lives because she wanted us to go on living a lie and… *Dios mio*, I wanted out!'

Molly was frowning. 'I don't understand. What was the truth?'

Leandro vented a harsh, unamused laugh. 'That she was gay. The moment she admitted it, I couldn't comprehend how I hadn't realised it for myself. She felt trapped in our life. Our marriage was a disaster, but she was willing to sacrifice both of us to keep her secret. At the moment she most needed my understanding and friendship, I turned on her and that's why she ran out, got in her car and ended up crashing it and killing herself.'

Molly was very much shocked and she reached out to grip his hands with hers. 'You must have been shattered and very bitter to find out after so many troubled years together. Of course you felt she had deceived you. It wasn't your fault she crashed, or your fault that your marriage didn't work. How could it have done? She was upset, Leandro. She must have been very unhappy. You both were. Let it go at that. Don't blame yourself for an accident.'

Leandro loosed his hands and bent down to lift her off her feet. 'You're always so considerate of how I feel and I honestly didn't know I had so many feelings until I met you, *mi corazón*. Uppermost was the pure erotic pleasure of a woman who wanted me just for myself,' he confessed huskily. 'Was it any wonder that I couldn't keep my hands off you?'

Molly blinked, still coming to terms with what he had shared with her about Aloise. He carried her upstairs and settled her on the big divan. 'I'm not any stronger. You're incredibly addictive,' she told him. 'I was a clean-living girl until you came along!'

Leandro gave her a rakish grin that tilted her heart on its axis. 'It meant a lot to me that I was your first lover. I think I fell in love with you the very first night we met, but I had no idea what had happened to me. Although I wasn't in love with her, Aloise hurt me,' he admitted gruffly. 'I tried so hard with her and got nowhere. I wanted to keep a distance with you, not get too involved, too close…'

Molly was transfixed by what he had said. 'You fell in love with me?'

'*Dios mio*…like a brick being chucked off the roof of a skyscraper. I'd never been in love before. In lust, *sì*. In love, never! But I couldn't tell the difference. The whole time I was in conflict with myself. I asked you to be my mistress.'

'And that hurt me.'

He crouched down in front of her, grasped her hands and kissed them in fervent apology. Her eyes shiny with love, her fingers smoothed his handsome dark head.

'It served you right that I was pregnant,' she told him. 'Why were you so careful to tell me that you couldn't give me love when you proposed?'

'I didn't know I had it to give. Love has never been my style. I was jealous of Jez for a long time.'

'Jez?' Molly yelped in disbelief.

'You and he had close ties that I found threatening,' Leandro admitted.

Molly rather liked the knowledge that Leandro wasn't as sure of himself as he always seemed. She leant forward and kissed him with loving brevity.

'Meeting you has been a humbling experience for me.' Springing upright, Leandro raised her and wrapped his arms round her in a possessive hold. 'I did everything wrong. I didn't give you the wedding or the honeymoon you should have had.'

'You were the bridegroom from hell,' his beloved confided without hesitation. 'But really great in bed after banking hours.'

'I love coming home to you—'

'But you were late back every night!' Molly complained, unable to let that claim go past unchallenged.

'I forced myself to play it cool, so that I didn't feel out of control,' he breathed. 'I *hate* feeling out of control.'

'I like it when you're out of control,' Molly whispered, ready to take shameless liberties with her exploring hands and then suddenly freezing in dismay. 'Oh, gosh, I still haven't told you about the birth control pills I found in the wardrobe!'

Leandro was astonished, but quickly realised they could only have belonged to Aloise. 'So, she didn't want children with me.'

'If she felt trapped in her life, a child would only have trapped her more,' Molly suggested.

'What does it matter now?' Leandro tugged her down onto his hard thighs and linked his hands round the swell of her belly with an air of proud satisfaction. 'It's all so long ago and you and I belong together. The minute I saw you I was drawn to you.'

Molly thought of all the years of feeling that she was not good enough for the people and the things she wanted and needed out of life. Her new-found siblings and Leandro had between them washed away all those wretched insecurities. Bubbling over with happiness at the new knowledge that she was loved, she realised that she owed him the same honesty.

'I only realised that I loved you the day I left the castle. Leaving broke my heart,' she confided.

'It took me far too long to realise what I was doing to you. When you walked out, I felt gutted,' Leandro admitted grimly. 'But it certainly did wake me up, *mi vida*. I had no idea you loved me.'

'Madly, passionately and for ever,' Molly swore with fervour and he surrendered to the glow of warmth in her eyes and kissed her with a passion that stole the breath from her lungs.

Eighteen months later, Molly walked down to the beach with Ophelia and her three children. The Greek island of Kastros, which belonged to her brother—Ophelia's husband—Lysander, was an oasis of perfect peace.

The latest addition to the family circle, little Felipe, slumbered in his all-terrain buggy. Black lashes as long as fly swats brushed his olive-skinned cheeks. With his black curls and green eyes, Molly and Leandro's firstborn was a handsome combination of his parental genes. A livewire toddler, usually he rarely slept during the hours of daylight. But they had had a barbecue on the beach the night before, which had kept him awake long past his usual bedtime and he was now making up for that.

Molly had given birth by Caesarean and made a speedy recovery. Felipe's birth had to some extent mended fences within Leandro's family. Thanks to Molly's intervention, Doña Maria had been allowed to attend her grandson's christening and had managed to be scrupulously polite to her daughter-in-law throughout the event. Her elder daughter, Estefania, was already a regular visitor at the *castillo*, having chosen to take her brother's side rather than her mother's when the family ructions were still at their height. Molly was under no illusions about the precise depth of her mother-in-law's warmth in her vicinity, but she preferred to tolerate occasional visits for the sake of peace and unity.

Julieta remained a close friend. The younger woman had long since got over her failed relationship with Fernando Santos and was currently dating a wealthy entrepreneur who seemed to think the sun rose and shone on her, and who had already gained Leandro's seal of approval.

Molly flew over to London regularly to meet up with her siblings and often made time to see Jez Andrews as well. Jez now had a girlfriend as committed to following the sport of motocross as he was and Molly fully expected to hear that Tamara would be moving in with him soon.

Molly's life in Spain had become frantically busy, which she loved. She had decided that the farmyard where her studio was would make a great craft village where local artists could work, exhibit and sell their wares. Financed by Leandro and by Nikolai, who had insisted on taking a financial stake in the concern as well, the concept had taken off like a rocket and had had the added benefit of providing a welcome local tourist attraction.

Once Molly had discovered just how much time and effort it took to run the *castillo*, she had hired an administrative assistant to take charge of the accounts. She had also given Basilio more power and used the older man's domestic expertise to ditch outdated working practices. Now Basilio was a much happier man. The household had come to run like clockwork and, furthermore, costs had been reduced, which had shocked and hugely impressed Leandro. The fact that his wife now spoke fluent Spanish had assisted her endeavours and she was very popular with the estate staff, who appreciated her practical, hard-working approach.

'There they are now...we should chuck rocks at them!' Ophelia pronounced with spirit as a Metaxis helicopter flew in and vanished from view to land behind her stunning contemporary Greek home. 'Lysander said he'd be back for lunch and it's almost dinner time.'

'Nikolai sent me a text saying that they had been delayed. Sorry, I forgot to tell you.' In the act of chasing after her three-year-old son, Danilo, and his toddler brother as they splashed through the surf, Abbey paused to speak in a tone of apology.

'Well, Nikolai wins in the communication stakes,' Molly acknowledged.

'Bet you anything he's put his name down on the waiting list for yet another wildly exotic car,' Nikolai's wife, the gorgeous red-headed Abbey forecast with a world-weary groan. 'We have garages full of cars. He doesn't even have time to drive them.'

'He just likes collecting them.' Molly lifted Felipe out of the buggy when he woke up with a cross little sob.

She began walking back up towards the stunning contemporary house above the beach just as the three men cleared the boundaries of the terraced gardens and began to stride down the hill to join their wives. Her heart leapt at the sight of Leandro's lean, darkly handsome face. Sometimes she loved him so much it hurt. And this was very definitely one of those times, when he was fresh back from the motor show that he had visited with Nikolai and Lysander. Unlike the other two men, Leandro couldn't have cared less about luxury cars. But in the interests of bonding with her brothers, he had made the effort to accompany them and fit in. These days the guys got on as well as their wives did, although being men there was a good deal more competitiveness and joshing in their dealings.

Felipe was opening his arms in greeting even as Leandro swept his son out of his wife's arms and high into the air. The little boy's shout of excitement delighted Molly. She loved the fact that Leandro was a real hands-on father. Tucking his son below his arm, he curved an arm round Molly.

'I missed you last night, *preciosa mia*,' he husked.

'Me too,' Molly whispered. 'We had a barbecue down here for the kids.'

Dark golden eyes nailed to her animated face, Leandro drew her close. Her lips tingled, heat rising in her cheeks.

'When are you two going to stop acting like honeymooners?' Nikolai quipped as he strode past them.

'Never,' Leandro breathed soft and low, unconcealed appreciation in his gaze as he continued to study his wife and wondered if she would like the very talkative parrot he had acquired for her in London. Ophelia had offered Haddock to Molly, but she hadn't liked to accept the parrot when Ophelia's children were so attached to the old bird.

Confidence and happiness were winging through Molly in a glorious wave. Later, when they were alone, she would tell Leandro that their second child was on the way and she knew he would be as overjoyed at that news as she was.

Felipe demanded to get down and examine the sandcastle being built by Poppy and her siblings. Molly looked at Nikolai, who was embracing Abbey while his sons clung to his trouser legs. Lysander was presenting Ophelia with a set of car keys and teasing her wickedly about some vehicle of his that she had crashed. Molly smiled again, loving the fact that she had a wonderful husband and such a loving and close family to share everything with…

* * * * *

Harlequin is 60 years old,
and Harlequin Blaze is celebrating!
After all, a lot can happen in 60 years,
or 60 minutes...or 60 seconds!
Find out what's going down in Blaze's
heart-stopping new mini-series,
FROM 0 TO 60!
Getting from "Hello" to "How was it?"
can happen fast....

Here's a sneak peek of the first book,
A LONG HARD RIDE
by Alison Kent
Available March 2009

"IS THAT FOR ME?" Trey asked.

Cardin Worth cocked her head to the side and considered how much better the day already seemed. "Good morning to you, too."

When she didn't hold out the second cup of coffee for him to take, he came closer. She sipped from her heavy white mug, hiding her grin and her giddy rush of nerves behind it.

But when he stopped in front of her, she made the mistake of lowering her gaze from his face to the exposed strip of his chest. It was either give him his cup of coffee or bury her nose against him and breathe in. She remembered so clearly how he smelled. How he tasted.

She gave him his coffee.

After taking a quick gulp, he smiled and said, "Good morning, Cardin. I hope the floor wasn't too hard for you."

The hardness of the floor hadn't been the problem. She shook her head. "Are you kidding? I slept like a baby, swaddled in my sleeping bag."

"In my sleeping bag, you mean."

If he wanted to get technical, yeah. "Thanks for the loaner. It made sleeping on the floor almost bearable."

As had the warmth of his spooned body, she thought, then quickly changed the subject. "I saw you have a loaf of bread and some eggs. Would you like me to cook breakfast?"

He lowered his coffee mug slowly, his gaze as warm as the sun on her shoulders, as the ceramic heating her hands. "I didn't bring you out here to wait on me."

"You didn't bring me out here at all. I volunteered to come."

"To help me get ready for the race. Not to serve me."

"It's just breakfast, Trey. And coffee." Even if last night it had been more. Even if the way he was looking at her made her want to climb back into that sleeping bag. "I work much better when my stomach's not growling. I thought it might be the same for you."

"It is, but I'll cook. You made the coffee."

"That's because I can't work at all without caffeine."

"If I'd known that, I would've put on a pot as soon I got up."

"What time *did* you get up?" Judging by the sun's position, she swore it couldn't be any later than seven now. And, yeah, they'd agreed to start working at six.

"Maybe four?" he guessed, giving her a lazy smile.

"But it was almost two..." She let the sentence dangle, finishing the thought privately. She was quite sure he knew exactly what time they'd finally fallen asleep after he'd made love to her.

The question facing her now was where did this relationship—if you could even call it *that*—go from here?

* * * * *

*Cardin and Trey are about to find out that
great sex is only the beginning....
Don't miss the fireworks!
Get ready for
A LONG HARD RIDE
by Alison Kent
Available March 2009,
wherever Blaze books are sold.*

HARLEQUIN *Presents*

ONE NIGHT BABY

When passion leads to pregnancy!

PLEASURE, PREGNANCY AND A PROPOSITION
by Heidi Rice

With tall, sexy, gorgeous men like these,
it's easy to get carried away with
the passion of the moment—and end up
unexpectedly, accidentally, shockingly

PREGNANT!

Book #2809

Available March 2009

Don't miss any books in this exciting new
miniseries from Harlequin Presents!

HARLEQUIN *Presents*

International Billionaires

Life is a game of power and pleasure.
And these men play to win!

AT THE ARGENTINIAN BILLIONAIRE'S BIDDING
by *India Grey*

Billionaire Alejandro D'Arienzo desires revenge
on Tamsin—the heiress who wrecked his past.
Tamsin is shocked when Alejandro threatens her
business with his ultimatum: *her name in tatters
or her body in his bed...*
Book #2806

Available March 2009

Eight volumes in all to collect!

HARLEQUIN *Presents*

*Introducing an exciting debut
from Harlequin Presents!*

Indulge yourself with this intense story
of passion, blackmail and seduction.

VALENTI'S
ONE-MONTH MISTRESS
by Sabrina Philips

Faye fell for the sensual Dante Valenti—but he
took her virginity and left her heartbroken. She
swore *never again!* But he wants her back,
and what Dante wants, Dante takes....

Book #2808

Available March 2009

Look out for more titles from Sabrina Philips
coming soon to Harlequin Presents!

THE BILLIONAIRE'S CONVENIENT WIFE

Forced to the altar for a marriage of convenience!

He's superrich, broodingly handsome and
needs a bride in name only....

She's innocent yet defiant, and she's about to be
promoted from mistress to convenient wife!

Look for all of our exciting books in March:

REQUEST YOUR
FREE BOOKS!

2 FREE NOVELS
PLUS 2
FREE GIFTS!

YES! Please send me 2 FREE Harlequin Presents® novels and my 2 FREE gifts (gifts are worth about $10). After receiving them, if I don't wish to receive any more books, I can return the shipping statement marked "cancel". If I don't cancel, I will receive 6 brand-new novels every month and be billed just $4.05 per book in the U.S. or $4.74 per book in Canada, plus 25¢ shipping and handling per book and applicable taxes, if any*. That's a savings of close to 15% off the cover price! I understand that accepting the 2 free books and gifts places me under no obligation to buy anything. I can always return a shipment and cancel at any time. Even if I never buy another book, the two free books and gifts are mine to keep forever.

106 HDN ERRW   306 HDN ERRL

Name	(PLEASE PRINT)	
Address		Apt. #
City	State/Prov.	Zip/Postal Code

Signature (if under 18, a parent or guardian must sign)

Mail to the **Harlequin Reader Service:**
IN U.S.A.: P.O. Box 1867, Buffalo, NY 14240-1867
IN CANADA: P.O. Box 609, Fort Erie, Ontario L2A 5X3

Not valid to current subscribers of Harlequin Presents® books.

Want to try two free books from another line?
Call 1-800-873-8635 or visit www.morefreebooks.com.

* Terms and prices subject to change without notice. N.Y. residents add applicable sales tax. Canadian residents will be charged applicable provincial taxes and GST. Offer not valid in Quebec. This offer is limited to one order per household. All orders subject to approval. Credit or debit balances in a customer's account(s) may be offset by any other outstanding balance owed by or to the customer. Please allow 4 to 6 weeks for delivery. Offer available while quantities last.

Your Privacy: Harlequin Books is committed to protecting your privacy. Our Privacy Policy is available online at www.eHarlequin.com or upon request from the Reader Service. From time to time we make our lists of customers available to reputable third parties who may have a product or service of interest to you. If you would prefer we not share your name and address, please check here. ☐

HP08R

I ♥ HARLEQUIN® *Presents*~

BROUGHT TO YOU BY FANS OF
HARLEQUIN PRESENTS.

We are its editors and authors
and biggest fans—and we'd
love to hear from YOU!

Subscribe today to our online blog at
www.iheartpresents.com